"WHAT WOULD YOU THINK IF DAD got remarried?" asked my older brother, Ian.

I had thought about that before. "I don't want another mother. . . . Maybe if she were nice, it would be all right."

"Megan's nice."

"Do you know something I don't?" I demanded, slamming down the paring knife.

Ian shrugged. "Just that Dad is really interested in Megan, that's all. . . ."

For adventure, excitement, and even romance . . .
Read these Quick Fox books:

Springtime of Khan
Summer by the Sea

Sports Books for Girls by Dan Jorgensen
Andrea's Best Shot
Dawn's Diamond Defense

Crystal Books by Stephen and Janet Bly
1 Crystal's Perilous Ride
2 Crystal's Solid Gold Discovery
3 Crystal's Rodeo Debut
4 Crystal's Mill Town Mystery
5 Crystal's Blizzard Trek
6 Crystal's Grand Entry

Marcia Books by Norma Jean Lutz
1 Good-bye, Beedee
2 Once Over Lightly
3 Oklahoma Summer

SPRINGTIME OF KHAN

Marian Flandrick Bray

Chariot Books
David C. Cook Publishing Co.

A Quick Fox Book

Published by Chariot Books,
an imprint of David C. Cook Publishing Co.

David C. Cook Publishing Co., Elgin, Illinois
David C. Cook Publishing Co., Weston, Ontario

SPRINGTIME OF KHAN

Cover design by Jill Novak
Cover illustration by Joe Yakovetic

First printing, 1988
Printed in the United States of America
92 91 90 89 88   1 2 3 4 5

Library of Congress Cataloging-in-Publication Data

Bray, Marian Flandrick, 1957—
    Springtime of Khan / Marian Flandrick Bray.
        p. cm.
    Summary: Freshman Emily Sowers knows she should
show Christian love and forgiveness for her spiteful enemy
Sarah, but she finds it difficult because Sarah persists in
mistreating the magnificent Arabian mare Emily hopes to
buy.
    [2. Horses—Fiction. 2. Animals—Treatment—Fiction.
3. Christian life—Fiction.] I. Title.
PZ7.B7388Sp 1988   [Fic]—dc19   88-19918
ISBN 1-555-13123-9

to Judy—I hope you have a Palamino to ride in Heaven

and special thanks and love to my critique group—
Maureen, Carol, and Marlys

Do you give the horse his strength
  or clothe his neck with a flowing mane?
Do you make him leap like a locust,
  striking terror with his proud snorting?
He paws fiercely, rejoicing in his strength,
  and charges into the fray.

Job 39:19-21

Contents

1
Monsters in the Grove

As we approached the fork in the narrow cattle trail, I slowed Cobol by setting my weight back and touching the reins. The three-year-old colt lifted his bay head, ears upright, listening.

"What do you hear?" I asked. He thrust his head higher, trying to snatch the bit, but halted when I pulled harder on the reins.

My brother Farley rode up, his legs against the shoulders of Bottom, our ancient gelding.

"Look at Bottom," he said. Bottom, like Cobol, arched his neck, ears forward. "I wonder what's over the hills."

One path rose up the swell of the hill while the other curled back down the small ridge we had climbed. I squeezed Cobol's sides and said, "Let's go up and see what's there."

"A' statement for living," said Farley, his face solemn, although his brown eyes were laughing. "Always strive to go up."

"You can't go up forever," I said. "Gotta come down sometime."

"Ah." He drummed his heels against Bottom's ribs,

and the gelding lumbered along. "There are many levels to that statement."

I grinned over my shoulder at him. Though Farley was only nine, Dad called him the household philosopher.

"Where did you get that idea?" I teased. "Off a Captain Crunch box?"

"You have no class, Emily. It was Cracker Jacks."

I clung to Cobol's mane as he leaped up the rutted trail, worn by many hooves. He was an honest colt, one who would give his all, and he picked his way quickly yet deftly to the top.

I loosened the reins, and Cobol strode over the flat hilltop, his black-tipped ears pricked south at the next row of hills.

"What do you hear?" I asked again. I patted his neck, warm under the tangled mane. I tried to comb it with my fingers. We'd been so busy at home that I hadn't had time to groom the horses the way I should.

Farley eased up alongside me. Bottom was still sticking his butterscotch-colored head high, snuffling at the air, watching the same string of hills as Cobol.

"I think it's a bear," said Farley.

"Bears don't live around here."

"Coyotes, then. Coyotes run down dogs and cats."

I didn't think there were as many coyotes as Farley liked to believe. He scooted closer to Bottom's bony withers.

"We'd better investigate," he said. "Could be a UFO landing."

"Now there's a solid possibility."

He stuck his tongue out at me. "It could be," he persisted. He let out a war whoop and slapped Bottom's hip. "Run, Bottom! Run! Monsters!" The gelding groaned and shifted into a canter, his buckskin body stretched out, straining, like an old ship with worn sails trying to catch the wind.

Colob pranced after him, tugging at the bit. I could almost hear the colt thinking, *Please, let's run, too.*

"Okay, let's move."

Cobol sprang. His long legs swept over the hilltop, churning up stalks of mustard flowers. One flower wrapped itself over my arm, and the sharp, earthy scent filled my head. I shook off the flower and leaned lower over Cobol's neck as he broke into a gallop.

Farley, bareback on Bottom, his legs tight against the gelding, swayed with each stride. Bottom gamely stayed in the lead, his left knee popping every few paces. Farley glanced back, and I gave him my narrow-eyed, speed-demon glare.

"Faster, Bottom, faster!" he called. Bottom flew, his heavy ears flattening, as Farley urged him on.

I tightened the reins, holding Cobol back. I wanted Bottom to win today.

As Bottom drew ahead, his whiskery nose out, Cobol yanked at the bit and tossed his neck, nearly pulling my arms out of the sockets. I held firm.

"You'll have other races," I explained to Cobol, but he curled his nostrils disdainfully. "I feel sorry for Bottom; he's old."

Bottom clomped ahead, leading by ten lengths. "Beat you!" hollered Farley.

I smiled. I was twelve when Mom and Dad got divorced two years ago, and it fell to me to look out for Farley—make sure he brushes his teeth, takes his lunch money to school, combs his hair, stuff like that. He's even more my responsibility since Ian, our older brother, started college last fall.

Bottom slowed near the grassy edge of the mini-mesa, and Cobol quickly caught up. Distracted from the race, Cobol stood with his ears straight up, listening on a frequency I couldn't hear.

11

"Farley's monsters?" I asked.

Bottom stared at me out of white-ringed eyes.

"Oh, no," I said. "It's fiery stallion time."

Bottom shied, snorting, his eyes bulging.

"Whoa, wild stallion," commanded Farley in a deep voice. Bottom whirled, head and tail up, his left knee popping.

Farley and I laughed. What a crazy horse! Dad used to team rope with him until a few years ago, although Bottom's real mission in life was to teach children to ride. To make them horse-friendly, as Ian would say. Bottom was the best riding instructor I'd ever had. Without him I'm sure I wouldn't be working green colts like Cobol for Dad.

A flock of birds, black with gem eyes, startled and spiraled up. Cobol flared his nostrils, sucking in the cool afternoon air, and stared—not at the birds, but at the fence of hills again.

"Let's go see," I said. I couldn't rest until I discovered what was going on over there. The horses dropped down the trail, tacking back and forth, sliding on their hocks. I forced Cobol to walk until we reached level ground, then trotted him to the hills. The wind snatched the horses' manes and tails.

When the horses crested the second line of hills, we drew rein. I shaded my eyes with my hand, searching, and played with my retainer, clicking it against my top teeth. "I don't see anything weird," I said finally.

"Invisible monsters," said Farley, and Bottom groaned.

"I agree with Bottom."

Farley stuck out his tongue at me.

We started down into the small valley that spilled between the hills, broken by a grove of oak trees. Bottom groaned again between puffing. *Slap, slap.* His hooves were big as platters. *Slap, slap, groan.*

"A new dance step," I said.

Farley swung his arms over his head, a graceful wreath. "We'll have to teach Ian so he can be suave with all his girlfriends."

"I'm sure he'd love that."

A chicken hawk soared above, winding down an unseen staircase, never beating his solid brown wings. A slight twist of his flight feathers and he rose back up, watchful and alert.

A thump, woody and deep, came off the valley floor. The chicken hawk didn't veer from his course, but Cobol and Bottom pricked up their ears, pointing them toward the grove.

"That sounded like someone kicking a box," said Farley.

We exchanged puzzled looks.

"Remember that bay filly who kicked down the stall door?" I asked. "That's what this sounds like."

I urged Cobol faster down the hill, and he moved willingly. Whatever it was couldn't be life threatening to the horses, because they have a strong sense of self-preservation. Maybe rams fighting? When sheep rammed together, their heads made booming sounds. Maybe a drug deal among the trees—muffled guns? A friend of Ian's used to be in a gang, and she said lots of deals went on where you'd least expect it.

The horses jogged side by side, rye grass swishing between their legs.

"I hope it's a unicorn," said Farley. "I've always wanted to see one."

"If it is, why are all the birds flying away? You'd think they'd want to see a unicorn."

"Maybe they don't know what he is."

Another flock of birds—dickey birds, Dad calls them—puffed up like a dusty cloud from the trees.

"Whatever it is," I said, "it's in that grove."

A breathy squeal floated to us.

"That sounds like a horse," I said, and put my heels into Cobol's ribs. Farley and Bottom galloped after us.

This was foaling season. Maybe a mare was fighting off dogs. I strained to listen above the hoofbeats, but couldn't hear anything else.

The grove loomed up. About twenty gnarled oaks hunched together, their branches a roof. I slowed Cobol and he crabstepped, his hooves crunching last year's leaves.

Another squeal. I was sure it was a horse. Then voices, male and female, but I couldn't catch their words.

"Who's in there?" I shouted. "What's happening to that horse?"

No answer. A sudden shuffle like something moving or struggling. Cobol hopped a fallen branch and burst through the trees into a rough ring of soft grass, glowing in the sunlight.

Where was the horse? There! In the shadows.

The horse shied and reared, hitting a branch with its head. Two people jumped away from the flailing animal. The horse crashed down with another angry squeal, landing square for a fraction of an instant; then its legs buckled and it dropped onto a bed of dead leaves.

"What are you idiots doing?" hollered Farley.

For a moment I thought the horse had broken its neck. It hung against the rope, gasping. Its halter was tied to the rope which was tied to a branch. Why didn't it get up?

I pulled out my pocket knife when someone stepped in front of me.

"It's only Emily," said a voice.

Sarah. Sarah Petersen. "I should have known," I snapped. "The creep of the century."

14

"Get out of here," said Sarah, crossing her arms over her chest. "This isn't any of your business."

"It's my business now," I said, dodging around her and sliding past her silent companion. He was a tall guy, who looked vaguely familiar. He could have stopped me, but he didn't. I snapped out the knife to cut the rope that was strangling the motionless horse.

2
The Rescue

I knelt next to the horse and touched its face. It drew its breath in ragged gulps, the rope tight against the halter. "Get up," I coaxed, tugging at the lead rope. "Why don't you get up?"

"I'm warning you, Emily," yelled Sarah. She strode toward me, her short, blonde hair bouncing. "Get away from my mare."

Her mare. I stared into the mare's eyes, dark and wide. "I'll free you," I said and began sawing at the nylon rope. My knife wasn't sharp, but I pressed hard. The mare didn't pull back, but instead watched Sarah draw near.

"That's *my* rope and *my* mare," said Sarah, putting her hands on her hips, which made her thin braclets tinkle. "Now get out of here."

I ignored her and kept sawing. Why didn't the mare rise—something must be wrong with her legs. I'd cut her loose, in any case.

A shadow moved, and Sarah slapped the knife from my hand. The blade flashed away, vanishing into dry leaves. Anger surged through me. Keeping my hand on the mare, I called, "Farley?"

Bottom's and Cobol's hooves shuffled through the leaves.

As Farley slid off Bottom, the guy took Sarah's arm. "Come on," he said in a low tone. "Let's get Khan and go."

"Yeah," jeered Farley. "Do what your boyfriend says and get out of here." He scrambled off Bottom, holding both sets of reins, and hunted for the knife.

"Leave the mare," I told them. "I'll take care of her, since you obviously can't."

Sarah leaned toward the boy and said, "Emily thinks she's God's gift to horses."

He didn't answer. I snapped, "Shut up. You and your push-button horses. You can't ride worth your salt."

Sarah started to retort, but the boy pulled her away.

I tugged at the mare again. What was wrong with her? She didn't groan or struggle as if she were in pain. Farley found the knife and tossed it to me. I sawed at the tough rope until my hand began to ache. The mare studied me, her velvet eyes following the motion of my hands. She looked as if she ought to be galloping on the desert sand, not tied to a dumb tree. With a square knot, no less.

I glanced up. Sarah and her boyfriend were whispering together, their blonde heads touching. "Who was the fool who didn't tie a slip knot?" I asked.

The guy held up his hand and said, "Look. This is a misunderstanding. Khan fell down and she won't get up. She's done this before."

"I'll say it's a misunderstanding," I said, frustrated because I wanted to get the mare away from them and the rope was taking forever to cut. "I'm not stupid. We heard this horse squalling two sets of hills back." Slight exaggeration—but Cobol and Bottom had heard her.

"Look," he said. His eyes—blue as Sarah's, only his

17

looked weary—were focused on my face. "We were trying to teach Khan to stand tied. She breaks every post in the place."

"Shut up, Nigel," said Sarah. "Emily, take your bratty brother and scram."

"I'm not leaving this mare!"

"Oh, heroics." Sarah threw her hands in the air.

"I'm not a brat, you space nerd," yelled Farley. "You should be space shot to Alpha Centauri."

Sarah glared at him, then said, "Emily and Khan deserve each other. They're both abnormal. Let's go."

The guy—Nigel—let go of Sarah's arm and stepped closer. His scent—sweaty, not unpleasant, but like Dad after he's worked hard in the sun—drifted to me.

"Look, Emily," said Nigel, his voice holding a touch of an accent. "Just back off and I'll get Khan to her feet."

I whipped the knife under his nose. "No way. Your horse training methods don't impress me. Can't even tie a slip knot. Of all the stupid. . . ."

Nigel's face darkened. "This is ridiculous," he muttered.

"Oh, let her take Khan and find out," shrilled Sarah. "She unties knots, rears, breaks rails. Have fun."

They marched over to their two horses, tied to another tree. Judging by the speed in which Nigel loosened the horses, he did know slip knots. He led the horses to Sarah, one on each side of him.

She took her horse, mounted, and rode up, shooting me a dirty look. Khan thrust out her face, mouth open, teeth wet, and Sarah's bay Thoroughbred jumped back. Sarah said in a cold, furious voice, "When you finish playing with Khan, bring her by my house. Along with a new lead rope."

They rode across the soft grass in the center, Nigel

astride a chestnut thoroughbred-looking horse with lots of white on its legs. I ran after them and shouted, "No way, you witch! This horse will never see you again."

Sarah and Nigel rode out of the grove. Cobol neighed as they disappeared.

"Want me to go after them?"

Farley sat, his skinny legs wrapped around Bottom's wooly shoulders, and he looked eager to ride out and—what? Do battle? I imagined Farley galloping up behind Sarah and Nigel with Bottom groaning and his knee popping. They would fall off their horses laughing.

But I couldn't tell Farley that. For a moment I forgot what a pest he could be, and a fierce love rose up in me. "No, thanks, Farley. They aren't worth it. Anyhow, we got the mare. That's what counts."

"Look at her. She's listening."

The mare stared at us with ebony eyes, not frightened or white-ringed, but levelly examining us. She held her head higher so the rope wasn't as tight.

"She's positively calculating," said Farley.

"Cereal box words?"

He grinned. "I told you. Cracker Jack boxes."

"Now, girl," I said and stood straighter. "Sarah's gone, so you can get up." I jerked at her halter. "Up!"

The mare blew out her breath, and to my surprise, rocked her weight back, braced her forelegs, and scrambled up in one fluid motion. She stretched out her neck and touched noses with Bottom. He popped open his eyes and sniffed.

"All right," said Farley. "She looks okay."

Cobol pranced at the ends of the reins and touched noses with the mare. She drew back and squealed. Cobol jumped, with a snort fluttering from his nose.

I faced Khan and she looked down at me. "Hello," I

said. She was taller than Cobol, probably close to sixteen hands, and her legs were long and clean except for scratches around her knees. A white, narrow scar curved over her left flank. She lowered her face and I blew softly in her nostrils, first one and then the other. She blew back, soft bursts of alfalfa-scented air.

"Maybe you can untie the rope instead of cutting it," Farley said.

I stood on my toes, one hand on Khan just in case she decided to move suddenly, and reached for the knot. "I bet Nigel tied it," I muttered. "Sarah couldn't reach this high. So he's the stupid one."

The knot was tight from the mare's weight, but I strained and the knot loosened. The rope slipped off the tree with a small shower of twigs.

"Time to go home," I told the horse. "You're right, Farley," I said and carefully swung up on Cobol, holding Khan's lead rope below the cut section.

"About what?"

"This horse was bluffing by falling down and not getting up." Sly creature. We rode out of the trees and Khan ponied as if someone had taught her how. She moved on her toes, springing lightly, her neck arched and her tail a gray curve to her hocks. An Arabian, but not a typey, inbred one.

"Remember that little orange Shetland?" asked Farley. "She was a bluffer."

I nodded. A friend from school had had a pony we tried to break to a cart, but she kept sitting down on the shafts. Every time we hitched her to the cart, she protested by shifting her haunch onto the shaft. We finally gave up because she was ready to break the cart! We never did break her to drive. "Animals are smarter than people think," I said.

"Dad will croak when he sees her."

"Don't worry about Dad. I can handle him," I

replied, to myself adding, *I hope*. He hated people who mistreated horses—something Sarah seemed to do often. She was beautiful, even I had to admit it. But her looks made the image of her hitting horses, like she did when her Thoroughbred took a wrong step or refused a jump, all the more out of place.

Sarah was always showing off and, because she was pretty, everyone watched. Unlike me. I look sort of mousey, with eyes too big for my face. Dad once told me I look like a lost puppy.

We rode down the long hill to our spread, as Dad calls it. Mom calls it a dump. She never used to call it that before she and Dad got divorced. I think she's trying to make us think we live in a lousy place, so we'll want to go live with her and Jack, the man she married. Never.

The sun faltered and shadows filled in, crossing over the triangle of our house and the two barns, one for trainees and one for boarders.

"There's Dad," I said and urged Cobol, the mare in tow, toward the boarders barn. Farley and Bottom rode near and when we stopped, outside a paddock, Bottom groaned. Dad straightened up from mending an automatic waterer.

"Hi, Dad," I said, in what I hoped was a bright tone. "Look what I found."

I held up the rope and the mare jerked her face high, her ears pricked and her mane falling back silvery over her neck. The chestnut in the paddock gyroscoped around and stuck his face over the pipe fence. Other horses came out of their stalls and into the paddocks.

"Where did you get her?" he asked, pushing back his John Deere visor. Apparently he passed Khan's inspection, because she lowered her head and Dad stroked her neck.

"From Sarah Petersen. You know, that snotty girl

who rides the bay Thoroughbred in shows?"

"She was torturing Khan," said Farley. "Sarah ought to be sent to another planet."

"Pity the people there," I said. Then I told Dad what had happened.

He slowly examined the mare while I talked, feeling Khan's sides and legs, sliding his big, square hand over her ocean gray coat. He studied the scratches on her knees and the thin scar on her flank. "Whip mark," he said. He lifted the nylon strap over her poll, and Khan ducked her head. "Beginnings of a rope burn."

I leaned closer to inspect the place. Her fur was worn and her skin red.

"I can put Bottom out in the sheep pasture and put Khan in his stall."

Dad's hazel eyes met mine. "Emily," he said, "this isn't your horse. You take her back to the Petersens'."

"Dad," Farley burst out. "That's criminal. Sarah was abusing Khan."

"Farley, go put Bottom away. Now. I'm behind in the chores and need everyone's help."

"Where's Ian? Why isn't he helping?"

Dad's mouth straightened. "I'll mind Ian. You just do as I say."

"Dad!" Farley gave me a mournful look, then a what-can-I-do shrug. He turned Bottom around and trotted to the other barn.

Dad slipped back into the paddock, shoving the chestnut horse aside and fiddling with the waterer. His head was sweaty where he was thinning on top. Cobol shifted his weight, playing with the copper rollers on his snaffle bit.

"What are you waiting for, Emily?"

"Dad! I'm not taking her back."

He raised his head. Cool. Very cool. I have to say that for my dad.

"Emily. That isn't your horse."

I leaned in the saddle, the skirts creaking. "Didn't you hear me, Dad? I can't take her back. Sarah was mistreating her. If I take her back she might do it again. Dad, Khan was tied—"

"I heard you fine," he broke in smoothly. "Now hurry and take her back to the Petersons'. And when you get back, start feeding the boarders."

"Dad! Cruelty to animals." I crossed my arms over my chest. "I won't take her back."

Dad came up to the fence. His eyes, usually a soft brown, were rock hard. "Yes, you will, Emily. And right now."

"But, Dad!"

He held up his hand and Khan shied, hitting the end of the rope. I grabbed it as it snaked over my legs. Khan snorted and bounded back.

"You scared her."

Dad gripped the fence and said in a solid voice, "I'm asking you once more, Emily."

"*O-kay!*" I put my heels into Cobol's sides, and Khan jogged behind. *Darn! How could he?* Cobol tried to turn back to his barn, but I booted his ribs and headed him down the road. The Petersens' ranch was about a mile away. From our place I saw their barn and the enclosed arena where Class A horse shows were held.

"I wish I were a horse," I muttered. "I'd like to flatten my ears and start kicking." I just couldn't take the mare back to Sarah. Maybe I could hide Khan. In the hills or at my best friend Melissa's house. She had an empty corral where her older brother had a steer last year. But I knew Dad would call the Petersens and check up on me, or Sarah would tell her father and he would call my dad. I was stuck.

"The worst part is that I told Sarah she'd never see

you again," I said to Khan. The mare raised her head and looked at me as if she knew what I was saying.

I always wanted a horse of my own. Just mine. One that would be a friend.

I put out my hand, and Khan sniffed at it. Sure, I could ride any of the horses in our barns, but that wasn't the same as having my own horse. I wanted a horse like Flicka was to Kennie or like The Black was to Alec. Both those horses loved their masters because their masters helped them when they were scared and hurt.

"I'm helping you," I whispered to Khan, but she didn't appear to hear. She just stared down the road to the Petersens' where Sarah, no doubt, was lying in wait for me.

I sighed. As a Christian I was supposed to love Sarah—yuck—but I didn't like her one bit. And I didn't want to like her either.

Ever since second grade when she moved here from hotty-totty, bluegrass Kentucky, she's been my enemy. I don't know why exactly. Maybe it's pheromones—we don't like the way each other smells.

The first day of second grade she tripped me. I fell in the aisle and everyone saw my underwear. I know she did it on purpose. Things have been more or less like that ever since, although at fourteen we're a little more subtle.

I rode Cobol past the white pasture fences. His hooves clicked on the pavement, but Khan's hooves, barefoot, made quiet thuds.

As I walked Cobol up the drive, gravel crunching under both horses' hooves, I hoped with all my might—was it fair to pray about this?—that Sarah wasn't home, that she was washing her hair, that she was doing something, anything, but waiting for me.

The two-story house spilled light across the garden

in the front yard. The sweet scent of roses surrounded me. Maybe I could put Khan in an empty stall or paddock before anyone saw me.

The horses were passing the house when a voice, all too familiar, sliced through the evening stillness: "That's my horse! She stole my horse!"

3
Star Language

Stole her horse! That was certainly one way to look at the situation. I slipped my retainer off my teeth and chomped on it, grimly reining in Cobol.

Two men walked toward me from the barn. Sarah broke her cover and ran up to Khan, grabbing the mare's lead rope. Khan half spun, recoiling against Cobol, and smashed my leg between her body and Cobol's.

"Ouch!" I pushed Cobol sideways and Khan followed. "If I stole your horse, what am I doing here?" I asked, rubbing my knee.

Sarah gave me a furious glare, her blue eyes narrowing. Before she could say anything, the men came over and stood in the bright vapor light from the barn. One was a wiry, thin man in tight jeans. The other, her father, was taller, more refined.

Sarah pointed at me and said, "Emily Sowers stole my horse."

Mr. Petersen tipped his head. The gold chains around his neck made him look like a coiffured dog—not a poodle, but an Airedale. Continental.

"I didn't steal Sarah's horse," I said. "I took Khan

away because Sarah and Nigel were abusing her."

"We were not. Emily ruined the lead rope."

"Only because you were strangling this mare." Fury swelled in me, and Cobol shifted nervously. I tried to calm down, if only for his sake.

Mr. Petersen sighed, a soft sigh, like one who had been through a similar situation before. Then he smiled, friendly and open, but I didn't trust him.

"Well, Emily," said Mr. Petersen, "there appears to have been a misunderstanding. I'll see to Khan. Mr. Dellins?"

The wiry man reached for Khan's rope. I whirled Cobol aside, and Khan neatly followed. Mr. Dellins froze, a hunting cat pose. I said quickly, "There wasn't a misunderstanding. Khan was being abused. And I want to buy her."

My words just tumbled out, and Sarah's mouth dropped in surprise. Any other time I would have laughed to see her so disarmed. Mr. Dellins folded his arms on his chest and glanced at Mr. Petersen.

Mr. Petersen's lizard boots crunched the gravel. "Do you know what this animal is worth?"

I could have guessed, but he continued, "Mr. Dellins is my top trainer. He bought this mare last month off the track in Florida for almost four thousand dollars."

I gulped and tried not to look too stunned. That was a lot of money, though I knew Arabians could go for much more. All I had in my bank account, representing years of hoarded birthday money and allowances, was just over five hundred dollars.

"She's not for sale, anyhow," said Sarah, her voice shrill. Cobol pointed his ears at her and flared his nostrils as if he was asking, *What kind of creature are you?*

Mr. Dellins half-smiled and reached for Khan

again. She sniffed at him, and I let the rope slide through my hands. He led her away and she followed docilely—Dellins must not be too bad a person. Khan's long tail swung back and forth as she clopped into a barn.

"Thank you for returning the mare," said Mr. Petersen, his voice firm. End of discussion. They headed for their house. Sarah's voice came to me as I guided Cobol down the drive, "Aren't you going to make her pay for the lead rope?"

"Why did she have to cut the rope, Sarah?"

I didn't hear her reply, but the triumph was shallow. She'd probably lie about what she and Nigel were doing. Poor Khan. I hoped Mr. Dellins would be nice to her.

I detoured home, taking Juniper Street where Melissa lived. I hurried; Dad would wonder what was taking me so long. Cobol shied at moving shadows in the deeper darkness when I rode up to the white stucco house. The sun was completely gone.

Upstairs in the wide attic bedroom that Melissa shared with her older sister, the light was on. Good. I halted Cobol under the plum tree and called, "Melissa." Soft rock music stirred out between the curtains. I called her name again. No answer. She was probably dreaming about my brother, Ian. Yuck. I broke a twig from the plum tree. Cobol jumped at the snap. "Steady, boy," I said and threw the twig against her window.

A face appeared. "Emily?"

"Were you expecting someone else?"

"Very funny. No one else I know is so weird. What do you want?"

"Why don't you come over to my house tonight, and I'll help you with your algebra?"

"Sick, Em. We just had a test today in algebra; don't

you remember? I need a break."

"Melissa, it's a ploy. I need to talk to you."

"Oh, I get it. Why don't you come over here?"

"I have a feeling Dad is going to corral me tonight. But he won't turn you away."

She laughed softly. "I'll see what I can do."

"Thanks. I gotta go. Chores await." I clucked to Cobol, and he turned in the grass.

"Is this about Stallion?"

"I wish." Stallion was our code name for this guy I was madly in love with.

Melissa laughed again. I guided the colt back on the main road. Melissa laughed a lot, but not without reason. She brought joy with her. I saw a quote somewhere that fit her perfectly: *Joy is the infallible sign of the presence of God.*

At the trainee barn, I put Cobol away. He buried his nose in alfalfa hay. I dumped a quart of cracked oats over the flakes. If I fed him grain straight, he'd gulp it and make himself sick. Patting his rump, I left him to dinner and stepped out of the stall.

Dad cruised up the aisle and handed me a shovel. "Mare home?"

"Yup."

He looked hard at me, then nodded, believing me. I got busy. Since the horses were closed in for the night, I had to work around them.

Farley dropped hay flakes into the mangers, and I heard Ian whistling. At least he was helping.

Ian pushed a wheelbarrel of dirty shavings past, stopped, and scooped up wet bedding that I had piled outside the stall door. His dark hair flopped in his eyes like a forelock. He was gangly looking, a colt just growing into his legs.

"Good evening, sister dear," he said.

"Shut up." Smart aleck.

He grinned and rolled on down the aisle.

As I cleaned the last stall, Farley perched on the Dutch door. "You should have heard the horses squeal for their dinner. It was funny."

"Move," I told a bony chestnut, pushing his shoulder so he sidestepped. I cleaned under him. Farley chattered on.

Dad appeared, coming to hang some halters on hooks beside the stall door. Farley jumped down, looking guilty. He wasn't supposed to sit up there.

Dad looked into the stall, his face lined and shadows smudging his eyes. I still thought I should have kept Khan, but I felt bad that I'd argued with Dad.

I peered out from under the chestnut's neck. "Did you get the waterer fixed?"

"Patched it," he said, leaning on the door. "But it's getting old. Like everything on this place. Thank God the pipe broke on the surface and not underground."

"Water everywhere?"

"It all ran into the ground as fast as it came out." Dad took off his visor, smoothed his hair, and pulled the cap back on. "I hate to think how much was wasted."

I didn't tell Dad that I had offered to buy Khan; he would think I was stupid with an A-plus. But I wanted to talk about her, to make her seem more real. "That mare was a race horse," I said.

"Really now?" Dad's voice was distant. He was probably thinking about pipes and cash flow.

"She is pretty," said Farley.

When Dad didn't respond, I said, "Farley and I can finish up here." Farley gave me a horrible grimace, but I ignored him. "You go and get cleaned up, Dad."

He smiled a small smile. "Thanks. I believe I will."

Farley and I finished mucking out the stalls and put the equipment away. Ian was back in the house, too, getting dinner. I told Farley about Khan going home.

"Maybe the trainer will keep Sarah from hurting her," he said.

I turned off the barn's interior lights. "I just hope she leaves Khan alone. Maybe she'll ignore her." I tried to give Sarah a little credit—very little—for behaving humanely.

Farley and I strolled across the dirt, past the bull pen where we break colts. The air was sharp and cold.

"There's Regulus," said Farley. Through the oak trees a star shone in the south, glittering and wild. "Know how far away it is?" He didn't wait for an answer. "Eighty-seven light-years. I wonder how it feels to be a star. A really old star, knowing you're going to turn into a white dwarf and die."

"Maybe stars go to heaven. Or transform into something else."

"God likes stars. He has names for all of them. I wonder what Regulus's real name is."

"Something special. God's into names."

"Yeah. Beautiful and in star language."

I smiled at him, but he was still looking up.

When we walked in the front door, I smelled spaghetti. Ian was the chef tonight. There's no question; he's the best in the family. We always gobble up everything he makes. Tonight was no exception.

"Growing children," remarked Ian, pushing his chair back from the table.

"Growing children, nothing!" said Dad. "I ate three platesful myself."

Ian leaned over and patted Dad's stomach, which is very flat, and said, "Growing in another direction."

Dad gave him a sour look, and we kids laughed.

Farley poked at the lime jello with his fork. "This jello," he announced, "is really an alternate universe."

Dad smiled, but Ian frowned. "Give me a break,

Farley. I don't make good cake, okay?"

"No, really," insisted Farley. "I'm not trying to be mean."

"You don't have to try."

"Inside every cube of jello is another world. Maybe we're in a cube of jello, too."

"As long as someone doesn't eat us," said Dad.

The doorbell rang. Dad's eyebrows knitted together. "Who could that be, Emily?"

"How should I know?" I figured it was Melissa.

Dad gave me a knowing look and went to answer the door.

4
Computer Talk

Melissa's voice came into the kitchen before she did. Ian gave me a lazy smile. "Your little friend is looking pretty good these days."

"Shut up, Ian."

Farley flicked a corner of jello at me. "Pow!" The jello stuck to the table top. "The ultimate weapon. Jello bombs. Goop up your enemy."

I laughed, enjoying a vision of Sarah bathed in lime jello.

Ian swung his leg over the arm of the chair. "Highly unamusing, children. But don't worry. I just won't cook anymore."

"Good," said Farley. "It stunts my growth."

"Brain growth."

Dad and Melissa walked into the kitchen. "Your pupil is here, Em," said Dad, giving me a suspicious glance.

Melissa grinned at me, then smiled straight at Ian. She's had a crush on him since seventh grade.

"Hi, Melissa," said Farley. "Want some jello?"

Ian ignored Farley, studying the ceiling.

"No, thanks, I just ate." She sat next to me in Dad's

chair and set her algebra book on the table. She shook the bowl of jello. "Is that what this is?"

"That's it," said Ian. "I've had enough." He threw down his napkin, but he didn't look mad.

Melissa winked at me.

"Dishes, Em," said Ian.

"No way. It's Farley's turn."

He squirmed in his chair.

"Look at the chart," said Dad. "It's all on the chart."

Every month Dad drew up a chart with our names and our chores. He was much more efficient since he and Mom got divorced. Our house was cleaner than many of our friends who had two parents.

"Homework for me," said Ian, untangling himself from his chair. Farley stared glumly at the chart.

"Didn't you have a test in algebra today, Emily?" asked Dad.

Melissa and I exchanged glances. Time to leave before Dad turned into full-fledged investigator. We needed a diversion.

"Ninth grade is a snap," said Ian, rubbing his barely-there mustache.

"Shut up, O Hairless One," I said.

He gave me a dirty look.

"Emily, don't tell your brother to shut up," said Dad. He stood in the middle of the floor, running his hands through his hair. The diversion was working.

Melissa and I got up and carried plates to the counter. "Get to work, Farley," I said.

"Don't tell me what to do."

Dad turned on the water. "Farley, come on. Don't make me tell you again."

Melissa and I vanished. I brushed my teeth and my retainer and heard Melissa open Ian's and Farley's bedroom door. The boys shared the master bedroom, and Dad and I have the smaller rooms. At first that seemed strange, because Mom and Dad had had that room forever, but I was used to it by now. I thought Dad was awfully nice to give up his room. "I don't need it," he had said. "You boys could use more space."

Melissa and Ian talked, their voices rising and falling. I pushed open the door. Ian's computer was glowing, and green letters skittered across the screen.

"See," he was saying. "I can bring up all the equations for the space telescope orbit. It's not too hard to figure out." He pressed a button, and the screen filled with a mass of equations.

Show off, I thought, but I didn't say anything. Melissa watched him the way I watch Stallion. With awe. Well, if she had to wash his stinky socks and brush cracker crumbs off his bed, she wouldn't be so amazed. But, looking on the good side, if she married Ian, then she'd be my sister-in-law. I'd like that.

I plopped down on Ian's bed. Melissa sat on the corner of the desk, Ian in the chair.

Farley's side of the room was cluttered and rumpled. The decor was pretty wild, because they argued for weeks about what color to paint the walls. Dad finally bought two colors, blue-gray for Ian and canary yellow for Farley. The colors neatly divided the room in half, ceiling too. It was terrible looking until you learned to ignore it.

"So what's going on?" Melissa asked me.

"It's about this horse," I began.

Ian interrupted. "Always horses."

Melissa kicked his leg. "Let her finish."

"Yes, ma'am."

Briefly, I told them what had happened.

"That Sarah," said Melissa, shaking her head. "What's going to happen to the mare?"

I chomped at my retainer. "Knowing Sarah, nothing good." I hesitated, then told them about my offer to buy Khan. They didn't laugh or say I was stupid.

Ian leaned back in his chair, balancing on the back legs. "Seriously," he said, "Petersen is a businessman. I doubt his daughter would hurt the mare. He's got vested interest in his livestock."

"Would you have really bought her?" asked Melissa.

I wasn't entirely convinced I wanted to spend my money on the quirky mare. But I didn't want Sarah to hurt Khan and, as much as I hated to admit it, a part of me just wanted to get the best of her.

"I think so," I said. "I wonder if I could make a deal with Petersen. You know how people, like thoroughbred people, share their horses?"

"Sure," said Melissa. "My brother owns part of a Brittany spaniel. He gets first pick of every litter if he wants it—except Mom won't let him. But our uncle sells her puppies, and they split the money."

"Exactly." I gazed at Ian's walls, which were covered with posters of space. Mercury, cratered and dead; Saturn, gleaming and bright ringed; galaxies —like freeze-dried fireworks—caught in the darkness of space.

Ian rocked in the chair. "But Petersen wasn't willing to sell?"

I shook my head. "He didn't give me a chance."

"You'd have to make him an offer he couldn't turn down."

"Whatever that might be." I sighed.

"Don't worry, sis. You can't save every abused animal. It's impossible."

"Maybe Sarah will be kinder, just knowing she was caught," suggested Melissa. "And you could ask that Nigel about the mare. Maybe he'll tell you."

"I doubt it. No reason for him to." I lay back on Ian's bed. They were being kind to me. I liked that, but they didn't have an answer. I yawned. I was more tired than I realized.

"What's that mare's name again?" Ian asked. There was an edge of controlled excitement in his voice.

"Why? What are you doing?" I struggled upright, I jumped off the bed, and looked over his shoulder. The terminal was alive, winking green, the cursor hovering in the far corner like a boxer ready to fight. Ian had his hand on the modem.

"They call her Khan. Why?"

"Ve have vays to make them talk," he said and grinned. "Why don't you shut the door, and we'll have a serious study session?" He grinned wider at Melissa, and she punched his arm.

I walked to the door. The radio was on, and Dad was rustling through the evening newspaper. Farley was still clattering dishes and making airplane noises in the kitchen. I shut the door quietly and returned to the desk.

The computer beeped regularly, and Ian stared at the screen, pressing an occasional button as jumbles of codes flashed on and off.

For a moment the screen read: PETERSEN BREEDING STOCK.

"This is sort of illegal, isn't it?" asked Melissa.

Ian shrugged. We all knew what Dad would say if he knew. "I won't change anything. We'll just see about the mare."

"Could you change grades?" she asked. "Because I have this bad feeling about that algebra test today."

"I could," he said. "But I won't. That's cheating."

"How noble," I said drily.

Ian lifted his hands from the keyboard. "I'll stop any time you want."

I elbowed him. "Go on." I used to want to be invisible so I could spy on people, but I didn't want them to be able to do that back to me. What a cheat I am. I had to know about Khan.

"Won't they know you've been in?" asked Melissa.

"I doubt their system's that sophisticated." He messed with the computer longer, then said, "Which horse is she?"

The screen heading read STOCK IN TRAINING. Underneath glowed a list of names, mostly foreign sounding. Two read KHAN JAFFLES and KHAN-NEAK.

"I don't know." I reached across Ian and pressed F-1 for the first name. "See what it says." The screen changed and Khan Jaffles came up.

    BAY STALLION   BLACK STOCKINGS
    WHITE BLAZE   FOUR-YEAR-OLD
    STOCK SADDLE   REINING HORSE

"Whoops," said Ian. "Not our mare." He changed the screen to the next horse.

    KHAN-NEAK   CHESTNUT MARE
    FIVE-YEAR-OLD   ENGLISH PLEASURE

"I'll go back to the menu and you pick the category," he said.

As the computer screen shifted, Melissa and I smiled at each other.

"Great algebra lesson," she said.

"Thank you. I thought you'd like it," I said.

"Algebra's nothing," said Ian. "Wait until you have calculus, symbolic logic. Good stuff like that."

"You'll have to wait a long time," said Melissa, "because I'm never going to take those classes."

The menus came up:

    FEEDS
    STABLE MANAGEMENT
    MARES: DRY OR IN FOAL

STALLIONS
ENGLISH SHOW HORSES
WESTERN SHOW HORSES
COMBINED TRAINING

"Mares," I said, "I know she's a mare."

We sorted through hundreds of horses, alphabetized by name.

"How can he have so many?" asked Melissa. "He hasn't room at his place."

"I think he has other ranches," I said. A series of Khans came up.

"The man's into Arabians," said Ian. "Recently, too." He pointed to the column of purchase dates. They were all within the last few years. After each mare, a string of sentences told about her: physical description, disposition, show record, breeding record, and more.

Ian kept pressing F-1. Finally a gray mare came up.

KHAN PIPPA   GRAY MARE FOALED AT
GREENROAD STABLES, FLORIDA

"I bet that's her," I said. "They bought her last month in Florida."

Her screen read on and on. She'd had twelve owners in her seven years. She'd even had one foal when she was four, but it had been stillborn.

The last entry was the purchase date and her race record:

FEB. 16 FLORIDA KEY RACETRACK
PURCHASED IN CLAIMING RACE.
BARRED FROM TRACK WHEN REARED
OVER BACKWARDS COMING OUT OF
STARTING GATE, REINSTATED TWO
MONTHS LATER.
FOUR STARTS. NO WINS.

"I didn't know they raced Arabians," said Melissa.

"It's big time," I said.

"She sounds like one spoiled horse," said Ian, leaning back in his chair.

"All those owers, never winning a race, and a dead baby, too. Poor mare." But I had an uneasy feeling about her. We looked at the rest of the Khans, just in case. Some were grays, but none matched up as well.

"They just bought her last month," I said. "She's still adjusting."

"Maybe she has jet lag." Ian grinned.

"Very funny."

Melissa glanced at her watch. "I've got to go. I told my mom I'd be home by eight-thirty."

Ian backed out of the program and switched over to his space orbit program. As Melissa jumped off the desk, Ian caught her hand. "Good-bye, fair maiden."

I pretended to gag.

Melissa yanked her hand free, her cheeks red. "You're crazy, Ian."

I opened the door. "Ignore him," I told Melissa. "His circuits need re-wiring."

Ian snorted. I walked with Melissa to the front door. Dad was still sitting at the couch, poring over the newspaper. He raised his head.

"Have a good study session?"

"Very informative," said Melissa.

"I bet," he said.

Melissa jogged toward her house. "See you at school," she called. I waved and shut the door, catching a glimpse of Regulus gleaming. Smothering a yawn, I came back to the couch. "I'm going to go take a shower," I said.

"Emily," said Dad. "Next time try asking if Melissa can come over. I really am a reasonable man."

"I do help her with her math."

"I know. But don't use it as an excuse. Remember the little boy who cried wolf?"

"Next time I'll ask."

On my way to my room, I impulsively stopped and poked my head into Ian's room. He was lying on his bed reading some book about black holes.

"Ian?"

"Hmm?"

"Thanks for looking up about Kahn. You didn't have to."

He lifted his head. "It's okay, Em. Just don't fret over that mare. She doesn't sound worth it."

"Maybe." I dug my toe into the carpet. "Ian?"

"What?"

"Your jello wasn't so bad."

He threw his pillow at me, but I slammed the door.

5
Hoofbeats at Twilight

The next day, during our fifteen-minute nutrition break, Melissa and I meandered across the student park. Kids sprawled on steps and benches and under trees, relaxing in the rare, hot spring sunlight. I swept my gaze through the crowd looking for Stallion. His real name was Don.

His voice, laughing, rough, in chorus with other voices, was louder than the static-y music pouring out of the square speakers hung on the outside cafeteria walls.

"Stallion alert," I hissed.

Melissa looked up. "Where?"

"By the B building steps." We started drifting in that direction, where Stallion lounged with some guys from the varsity football team. Although football was over—they were all playing varsity baseball this season—they were top dogs on campus.

"Would your dad ever let you date him?"

I laughed. "As if he'd ever ask me."

"He might some day. I bet your mom would let you go out with him."

"Yeah. Especially if he has money. My mom has a

one-track mind." I took my brush out of my backpack. "Wait." I had braided my hair last night so it was crinkled. I brushed hard, then stuck the brush back in the pack.

We strolled on. Actually, the only time Stallion had ever talked to me was last summer before I was even in high school. A snippy dun mare had bucked me off. We were out in the middle of nowhere when she unloaded me and took off running. Then Stallion had appeared like a mirage.

"Are you hurt?" he had asked, helping me up. I can still feel his fingers on my arm. He had on jogging shorts and smelled like moist sunlight.

"I'm fine," I had said, blinking back tears, mostly because I was mad. "I've got to catch that fool mare."

He helped me chase her down (she was knee deep in rye grass, the greedy animal) and held the reins when I mounted. I was in love from that moment on. Talk about a knight in gym shorts.

Unfortunately, when school started he didn't recognize his princess. He didn't even say hello. I learned his class schedule and where his locker was and managed to appear several times a day. You'd think he'd finally remember me by now.

"Maybe it's because you've matured so much," said Melissa, guessing what I was thinking.

"I haven't matured *that* much." I rolled my eyes.

She giggled and I laughed with her. Sitting under a tree directly across from Stallion and his buddies, I said, "I suppose it's hopeless." I peeled an orange from my backpack and offered a wedge to Melissa.

"Have you seen Sarah today?" she asked.

"No," I said. "It's a good thing, because I'd like to beat her face."

"Was your dad mad that I was at your house?"

"Not really." I glanced up; Stallion was watching

us. I sat ramrod still. "Melissa," I said in a strangled voice. "He's staring at me."

"Who?" She started to turn and I kicked her leg.

"Don't look, stupid. Him. Stallion." She had her back to the B building. I pretended I was looking at her, then I tipped my head slightly, gazing beyond her. My eyes met his. I dropped my gaze to the grass. "He's still looking."

"Wave to him. Smile."

"I can't. Maybe he's not really looking at me; then he'll think I'm stupid."

She started to turn, but I grabbed her shoulders. "Don't you dare."

We started giggling. The passing bell jangled. Stallion stood and stretched. He had big muscles on his arms like Dad. Casually he dropped down the steps, springing, smooth.

"Get up," I hissed. "He's coming this way."

We hopped up. My heart was pounding so hard, I could hardly breathe. I hoped he would say hi. I'd say, *I remember you. You saved me from that wild horse.* I almost laughed. Wild horse, indeed.

I pretended I wasn't thinking of anything except the cool breeze blowing across the lawn. Kids jammed the sidewalk, but Melissa and I stayed on course.

"T-minus five seconds," she whispered.

Stallion and I would walk right next to each other. Maybe he would smile at me, touch my arm. My skin remembered his touch last summer and tingled.

We were only a few feet apart. All the movies where lovers run into each other's arms flooded my mind.

"T-minus two seconds," said Melissa.

"Shut up!" I snapped.

The crush of kids grew. Everyone seemed headed for the B building. Stallion was still looking at me.

Stallion was two strides away. My gaze passed over

his face. What green eyes! My lips twitched into a smile. *Hello*, I practiced once more in my mind. I opened my mouth to greet him when a voice in my ear said, "Emily."

I stared dumbly at Stallion. His mouth hadn't moved. What was he? A ventriloquist?

He walked past. I wanted to touch his arm, but someone grabbed my elbow and pulled me off the sidewalk onto the grass.

"What the—" I whirled and faced the guy who had been with Sarah and Khan. Nigel. His face was smooth angles, his eyes light blue, yet a brooding quality surrounded him.

"I was about to talk to someone I never get to see," I said furiously. I didn't even know if Stallion was still looking for me. I couldn't see him in the crowd.

"Sorry."

"I bet. So what do you want?"

"Simmer down." His voice hardened to match his eyes, frozen blue. Again I detected that curious, faint accent.

Putting my hands on my hips, I glared at him. "So, I'm calm. What do you want?"

"I wanted to tell you that I wasn't trying to hurt Khan. I was dumb about the knot, but that mare can untie slip knots. You just happened to ride up when she decided to fall down. It looked worse than it was."

I stared at him. "I don't think so. Khan had scratches on her legs and the start of a rope burn."

We glowered at each other a moment. I expected Nigel to protest, but he said nothing more. His face closed up and he walked away, sliding in with the rush of students, lost to the crowds.

Fine, stalk off. A pinprick of guilt stabbed me.

"He didn't look too happy," said Melissa.

"Neither am I. And I've got to go to my locker."

We hurried upstairs to the C building, where I grabbed my algebra book and we raced for class.

"That Nigel," I fumed as we ran. "I could have talked to Stallion."

Melissa slowed, her shoes clicking in the almost empty hall. She gave me a weak smile. "Actually, he stopped and talked to Nadine. She was right behind us."

Nadine. The student body (emphasis on body) president. I stared at my notebook, feeling stupid. As if Stallion would ever pay attention to me, little freshman, ordinary looking. "I guess it was a good thing I didn't say hi."

"I think so."

We slid into the classroom as the tardy bell rang. Mr. Hart looked over his glasses at us, but only said, "Class, pass your homework forward."

Mr. Hart kept us busy copying formulas, but my head was full of Stallion and Nigel and Sarah—the last of whom sat across the room, directly in my line of vision. I chomped my retainer, like Cobol chewing his snaffle bit, until Melissa jabbed me with her pencil.

When the school day finally ended, Melissa and I got our books and started home. The wind blew my hair into my mouth.

"Do you want to ride?" I asked.

Melissa sighed. "I have to help my mom. Brenda is going to this fancy dinner, and Mom's making her dress. Guess who's the little helper?"

"Too bad. I thought I'd spy out the Petersen ranch and see if they're beating Khan."

"And if they are, then what? You'll ride down and rescue her?"

"I will. I'll raid the place, and this time I won't give her back—no matter what Dad says."

"Thou shalt not steal."

I stuck out my tongue. "This is different."

"Hardly." Melissa took a swing at me, but I jumped out of the way. "Maybe you should talk to Mr. Petersen again," she said.

The winds curled dust devils along the road. "I just don't get it," I said. "I'd like to think the best about people. Supposing Nigel is a nice guy, and there *was* just a misunderstanding about what I saw. But if Nigel is a nice guy, why does he hang out with Sarah the creep? That doesn't match up."

"Maybe Nigel could be super nice, and he's trying to be friends with her."

"Or Nigel isn't nice and Sarah isn't nice, and they're both lying about Khan."

"Or Nigel is super nice, and Sarah is really nice underneath."

I made a face. "Don't make me sick."

Melissa chuckled. We had reached her yard, and Cobol's hoof prints were still evident in the dirt and grass under her bedroom window. "We could pray about it," she said. "Not to be pious or anything, but it does work."

"Now? Here?" I've been a Christian for about a year and a half, but I'm not much in the habit of praying. Melissa is more experienced; she was saved when she was a little kid.

"Sure. And if my mom looks out the window and sees us, extra bonus. She'll think I'm getting more spiritual, and that'll make her happy."

I smiled. Melissa sounded smart aleck-y, but I knew she was teasing. "Why don't you pray," I said. "I don't know what to say."

We sat on the split rail fence and closed our eyes. Melissa's words fell softly, a good rain. "God, show Emily what she ought to do about Khan. In Proverbs

47

you talk about taking care of animals. So help Emily to do that. Thanks, God. In Jesus' name. Amen."

The wind touched my throat as I opened my eyes. Melissa was staring thoughtfully in the distance.

"Oh," she said. "I forgot. Close your eyes again."

I pressed my hands over my face, and Melissa added, "P.S. God, please help Emily to love her enemy, Sarah." Then she started running for the house.

"Sneaky!" I exploded off the fence and chased after her. *Love Sarah!* What a joke. I poured on the speed and overtook Melissa at her door. I grabbed her arm and spun her around. She was laughing.

"Love your enemies," she said primly and yanked free.

"Thanks for the advice," I said. "Have fun dress designing."

She groaned and opened the front door. "My sister is so picky." As the door was shutting, her voice rose a scale, "Why, hello, Brenda. I meant, you're such a perfectionist!"

"Don't believe her, Brenda!" I called as I left.

I puffed up the hill to our place, changing into my jeans, and ate a slice of bread and peanut butter before going out to the barn.

Beginning with the boarders barn, I raked pens. After I rode a colt, I'd return to feed, do more chores, and then start my homework. Yuck. Not too much homework though, because spring vacation started after Friday.

I raked fast, piling horse apples, as Mom used to call them, out in front of each stall. Once a week the local nursery came for the manure. How do beautiful sweet peas, moon flowers, and tulips grow from that? God's mysteries, I guess, like Pastor Tom talks about. I have a feeling manure and flowers wasn't quite what he meant, but it's nonetheless true.

I cut across the dirt to the trainee barn and blew at Cobol. He blew back, warm and molasses-y.

"Today I have to ride Io," I told him, giving him a final pat and heading for the chestnut colt's pen.

Ian had named Io (and Cobol, too, for that matter). Io is the moon closest to Jupiter, and volcanoes explode across its surface, even though the temperature is -200°F. And Io, the horse, is half Thoroughbred, restless and explosive.

The colt greeted me by turning around, ears up, eyes stretched to show the whites. I crooned to him for a few minutes, so when I opened his stall door he just heaved a sigh and lowered his head. I tacked him up, but before I mounted, I darted into the tack room for Dad's binoculars and tied them around my waist. Then I mounted Io and pointed him toward the hills.

He took long fast strides, his body tight with excitement, his head high, sucking in scents, sharp sage and new grass shoots. I settled him on the five mile path, up through the hills, down River Canyon Road, where the path poured out above the Petersens' ranch.

According to Io's owners, he was to be a Western show horse, whether he was suited or not. Of course they never asked my opinion, but with his leggy, Thoroughbred look, I thought he'd be a nice hunter or maybe an endurance horse. Who knew what was locked inside him?

We soared through the hills, the wind grasping his mane and my hair. He spooked at a chicken hawk lurching up from the ground. "Easy," I murmured. He snorted out the scent. Chicken hawks were scavengers with ugly, vulture faces.

The dirt road turned to broken pavement at the top of the hill above the Petersens' ranch. The sun was laying down stripes of red and gold over the barns and corrals. I halted Io and untied the binoculars.

The image telescoped close. I saw horses attached to hot walkers. Some Arabians. Dished muzzles, arched tails. No grays. I couldn't see into the covered arena, however, and horses and riders moved in and out of it. Someone with gold hair on a bright horse popped out, then back in. Sarah?

Io stamped a foreleg. "Okay, I get the message." I exercised him, figure eights, posting on both diagonals, little puffs of dust fluffing up from his hooves. I pushed him into a lope, being sure he picked up the proper lead. He messed up a few times. Most horses are left hooved, and Io didn't like his right lead. I tipped his nose to the left, giving him strong leg pressure with my left leg, and finally he cantered on his right lead, then executed a figure eight, doing two flying lead changes.

"Perfect!"

He pranced in place and I let him be happy. While he crowed over himself, I looked through the binoculars again. More shadows clung to the back half of the ranch, and the red and gold faded. Someone rode out of the arena on a red horse with splashy white legs and began an outside jump course. The horse cleared every jump neat as an arrow. Io, head up, listened to the regular thud of hooves.

Another horse and rider came into the arena, and the white legged horse stopped jumping. As the sun oozed the last of its light along the horizon, I could only see darkish outlines.

Io stamped his forefoot again. "Okay, let's go." I was disappointed that I hadn't seen Khan. As we rode away the regular hoofbeats started up again. Jumping a horse in the dark? Stupid.

Halfway between the Petersens' and Melissa's, Io looked back, his nose thrust out, pointing in the gray dusk.

50

I didn't see headlights or hear an engine. A dog? Io spooked, jumping sideways. I grabbed the horn of the saddle as his hooves struck the street. He whirled around as I heard rapid-fire hooves behind us. In the dying light, a horse raced up the road after us, stirrups ringing and reins flapping, whipping the animal on.

6
Rescue
Number Two

Galloping on the shoulder of the road, the horse didn't slow down as it approached. I backed Io out of the way as faint voices shouted behind. The horse closed in.

Io whickered and the horse hesitated, then shot past. Impulsively, I sent Io into a gallop after it, and as he accelerated, I leaned forward, unsnapping his lead rope and unknotting it from his neck.

We raced up the hill toward home, Io stretching out, his stride sure, his hooves cupping the soft shoulder. As we came up alongside the horse, it looked sideways at me, ears flat, eyes large and dark.

Khan. Somehow I wasn't surprised.

"Whoa, girl, whoa." I started to reach for her, but she gave me a wary look and moved out of arm's reach, still galloping. I shoved Io closer and Khan moved again, her hooves striking asphalt. Terrible for her legs, but better than tripping over mailboxes and trashcans hidden in the dark. Io's shod hooves hit the street, sending sparks into the night. Leaning over, I grabbed Khan's headstall. She ducked, but I held tight and gathered in the flapping reins.

"Whoa, whoa." She jerked back and half-hauled me from the saddle, the street an endless pit below me. Digging my knees in, I regained my seat and began to slow Io. I pulled Khan's head over my lap. Both horses ran a few more strides, then slackened their speed. Khan breathed hot air on my arms, and her nose dripped circles of moisture onto my jeans.

Snapping the lead rope onto both of the snaffle bit rings, I said, "Steady, Khan, Io." Finally Io dropped to a walk and craned his head around to sniff at the mare.

Khan pranced and pulled her head off my lap. "We're going home," I said, not waiting for the men whose voices I heard behind us. *Fools. Couldn't control Khan.*

As the mare trotted beside me up the hill, she bobbed her head with every other stride. In the darkness I couldn't tell which leg she limped off.

"Walk, walk," I said and pulled on the rope. She half reared, stumbled and, coming down with a grunt on all fours, tried to bolt. I dallied the rope around the saddlehorn, hoping the bridle wouldn't break as she jerked back.

Our house glowed, an oasis in the darkness. Through the curtains I saw Ian in his bedroom, working at his terminal. I stood in the stirrups and shouted.

"Ian!"

Khan plunged at my voice but bounced back, tossing her head, grinding the bit between her teeth.

Ian came to the window. "Em? What are you doing?"

"Where's Dad? I need him to come to Bottom's stall. Hurry. You, too."

"What are you doing?"

"Never mind. Just get Dad and hurry."

I rode to the boarders barn and dismounted, grabbing another rope and tying Io to the rail. I held

Khan, remembering what Nigel had said about her breaking posts—Dad would be furious if she snapped the railing—and she limped after me. I hauled Bottom from his stall. He looked offended. "Sorry, fella." I tied him at the opposite end of the rail from Io. Bottom snuffled Khan as I tied him, and she raised her hind leg, squealing.

"Stop." I bumped her under the chin and she flattened her ears, backing up. "Come here," I said, pulling her to me. She took a step, eyeing me uneasily, and I met her halfway and stripped off the dressage saddle and D-ring bridle. She had probably unloaded a rider. I led her into Bottom's stall.

Dad, Ian, and Farley appeared and looked over the stall partition.

"Why are two men in a jeep driving up? And a boy on a horse riding up?" asked Dad in his I-know-what's-going-on-but-I'll-let-you-tell-me voice.

"They're chasing Khan," I said, my voice trembling a little. "She ran away from them, and I caught her. I'm not returning her this time!"

Khan held up her leg, bearing her weight on her forelegs and her near hind leg. Long skinny welts rose up in her gray coat.

Dad opened the stall door and quietly came in. "Ian," he said over his shoulder. "Would you let the gentlemen know where their mare is?"

I stared at the pine shavings.

Dad felt Khan's chest. "She's fairly cool for galloping around the countryside."

"But she's shaking." I felt miserable.

"Farley, go and get a blanket," said Dad. Farley vanished in the direction Ian had gone. Dad ran his hand down Khan's neck and ribs and to her off hind leg. "I bet she went down," he said. The mare held herself taut, ears back as though she were thinking about kicking Dad, but he stood close enough that she could only shove at him. "See how her hocks have hair missing? I'd guess she went over backwards."

"She reared when I was ponying her," I said. I didn't want to admit she had a dangerous habit, but I had to be honest.

Farley reappeared with a blanket. Dad carefully spread it on her back, folding the cotton away from her split hip which bled a thin trickle down her haunch.

"Not a good thing, rearing," he said. Khan flicked her ears at him. "She has that rope burn behind her ears. That might make her rear."

"Someone has been hitting her." I pointed to the welts.

"After we talk with the men, we'll clean her up. She's pretty jumpy," Dad said.

My heart soared. Maybe he was coming over onto my side.

An engine roared and stopped outside. Voices rose and fell angrily. Khan flattened her ears, and I tightened my grip on the halter.

Suddenly a man I didn't know looked into the stall, his face ferret-sharp. "Here the beast is," he said. Then Mr. Dellins looked in. Behind them came a horse and rider. Nigel. His horse was a big chestnut, and when it pawed I saw its white forelegs. *So you're not involved in abusing her*, I thought. I regretted ever thinking he was innocent.

"Sorry for the trouble," said Dellins, in a smooth, clipped voice. "I'll just take her now."

Dad stepped through the shavings. "Wait a minute. This mare isn't going anywhere. She's lame and needs to be trailered. But on top of that, my daughter could have been seriously hurt because of your horse running loose in the night."

Mr. Dellins gave a delicate sigh. "I'm very sorry," he repeated. "I'll call for a trailer." He made it sound like Dad was a child to be pacified.

Dad clenched his jaw so the veins in his neck popped up. We kids had learned to vanish when he looked like that, but Mr. Dellins wasn't that smart.

"Not to mention the whip marks and injured hip on this horse," Dad continued. "I thought you people were trainers. I think the SPCA or the International Arabian Horse Association would be fascinated by this."

"You don't know what you're talking about, sir," said Mr. Dellins.

"My name is John Sowers. I've trained horses here for more than twenty years." Dad's voice was laced with fury. I was shocked to realize it wasn't just Sarah who treated me second class—grownups actually did that to each other, too.

"Okay, Sowers." His voice softened, but I didn't trust him. "This mare is hot off the track and higher than a kite. She went over backwards with my rider." Dellins gestured to the silent men, whose face was a dark mask.

The rider muttered, "It ain't the first time, either."

Nigel still sat on his horse. Our eyes met, and I refused to look away. *Creep. Abusing horses.*

"I don't care," said Dad. "You don't treat horses, any horse, like this." He waved at Khan's injuries. Mr. Dellins didn't change expression. Nigel looked away, smoothing his horse's mane. "You tell Mr. Petersen that if he'd like his horse back, he'd better come personally and speak to me."

Mr. Dellins heaved another sigh. "Very well," he said and sharply turned, heading for the jeep. Nigel wheeled his horse around as I leaned against Farley, watching Nigel ride away, his horse's white legs flashing in the barn lights. So he was the one jumping a horse in the dark. Fool.

The jeep roared off and Nigel cantered away.

Ian hung over the stall door. "Way to go, Dad!"

Dad laughed mirthlessly. "I should have punched Dellins out. I've wanted to for years."

"Dad!" I said, shocked but delighted. "You should have!"

He ruffled my hair. "It would have gotten me into trouble."

"So now what?" asked Farley.

"Wait for His Highness," I said.

"Really, Emily. Bill Petersen is a sharp businessman. I have respect for him."

I held Khan while Dad checked her more carefully. He sent Farley running for a bucket of warm water and a soft rag, one of our old baby diapers. Gently he cleaned Khan's cut. She held still, turning her fine head at him, watching him move around her.

She reminded me of a colt we had in training a couple of years ago. He had fallen and gashed his leg just above the hoof, right to the sesamoid bone. He'd been in pain, limping and shuddering, but when the vet drove up, that colt let out a ringing neigh, as if he was saying, *Where have you been?* Khan seemed to know we were helping her.

"See?" I told her. "We're your friends." She fluttered her nostrils.

Too soon Mr. Petersen roared up in his shiny black truck.

"Nice truck," said Ian. "Very nice."

Farley scrambled up on top of the stall divider and swung his skinny legs back and forth. Dad glanced at him, but for once didn't tell him to get down.

"Sowers," said Mr. Petersen in a neutral voice as he climbed out of the truck. *Good actor*, I thought.

"Hello, young man," boomed Mr. Petersen to Farley. I turned away to keep from laughing as Farley gave him an I'm-just-a-dumb-kid smile.

" 'Lo," said Farley, still swinging his legs. Ian lurked nearby, his shadow crossing the slated wooden walls.

Dad handed me the plastic bucket and wiped his hands on his jeans. "How are you, Bill?" They shook hands across the door.

Mr. Petersen caught my eye. "Emily. Looks like you've got my mare again."

I swallowed. "I guess I do." I felt like adding, *And I'm not giving her back*.

"A problem here," said Dad in a conversational tone. "This mare was running loose, and Emily happened to catch her."

Mr. Petersen tipped back his head. "I hear she takes it in her head to throw riders. I'm sorry about her getting loose. I'll have to clamp down on my men."

"She's quiet now," said Farley.

"A ploy," said Mr. Petersen. "It's too bad she's like this. My daughter thought she'd be able to work with this mare, but that's out of the question."

Dad raised his eyebrows at me. I took a deep breath, not looking at Dad or my brothers, but fixing my gaze on Mr. Petersen. "Sir," I said. "I'd like to offer to buy this mare, since she's a problem for you."

A flicker of annoyance crossed his face. I didn't dare look at Dad.

"Honey, I told you what this mare's worth. Can you afford that?"

My face burned. "I hoped we could strike a bargain. I'd take her off your hands, since she's causing so much trouble, and give you five hundred dollars, cash, tomorrow after I get out of school. I'd also give you her first foal. I'd gentle the baby myself."

He gave a laugh. "Well, John, you've got yourself a horse dealing daughter."

I gripped Khan's lead rope tighter and ventured a glance at Dad, who was rubbing his head under his visor.

"You're right, Bill. But I never knew it."

I couldn't tell what Dad was thinking. But he always said he was trying to get us kids ready to meet the world. Being grown up meant making decisions, right? So I was deciding to rescue Khan.

Mr. Petersen rested his arms on the stall divider next to Farley. "I spend good money on that mare, Emily. Buying her, shipping her across the country."

He was taunting me, treating me like a dumb kid. Of course I knew Khan had cost him money. "You'd get your money back from her first foal," I said. "It'll be easy because the foal will be gentle. I'll see to that."

"Where will the stud come from?"

My face burned again. "One of your horses. We've only a Quarter stud here, and he isn't much to look at. Besides, you'd want a purebred foal out of Khan."

I looked sideways at Dad, who finally met my gaze. His brown eyes were bright, as if he were enjoying a joke, but I didn't think he was laughing at me. He must be liking the fact that I was dealing with Mr. Petersen. I felt better, knowing he was on my side.

Mr. Petersen shifted his weight and hit the door, clanging the latch. Khan started, but settled down when I spoke to her softly.

"I'll be honest," said Mr. Petersen, but I wondered if he was being truthful or just thought he was. "That mare has been causing trouble the whole month I've had her. Broke some rails. Landed kicks to my stablehands. Now this rearing and rolling on her rider. You're welcome to her, Emily, if your dad says you can buy her. But I won't take her back if she acts wild with you, and you'll have to hold to your end of the bargain with the foal."

I turned eagerly to Dad.

"Is that fair, John?" Mr. Peterson continued. "She's as temperamental as they come. She was barred from the track because she reared and flipped over. Personally, I think the jockey was too heavy handed. I saw the video of the race, and she shouldn't have gone over backwards."

Dad thrust his hands in his pants pockets. "I don't know much about Arabs, but I think a horse is a horse. With some care, she ought to come around."

Dad and Mr. Petersen stared at each other a moment, the way dogs stiffen and gaze at each other before attacking. But Dad said calmly, "Emily's getting old enough to decide what to do with her time and money." He glanced at me. "So it's all right with me for her to buy this mare."

Mr. Petersen gave a quick nod. "Drop by my office, and we'll sign the papers."

Thanks, God. I wanted to jump up and down and throw my arms around Khan's neck, but I didn't want to upset her. I wanted Khan to know I was her friend.

"After school," I said. "I'll bring the money then."

"One more thing," said Mr. Petersen. "I can't hold you to this, Emily, but I wish you and Sarah could be friends. I know Sarah can be difficult, and she's been more that way since her mother's gone. But I'd appreciate it if you'd give it a try."

The color drained from my face. Be friends with Sarah? Mr. Petersen and Dad were staring at me, waiting for an answer. I said quickly, "Sure. I'll try that."

"Thanks. See you tomorrow." Mr. Petersen climbed into his truck. The headlights stabbed the night and the engine gears shifted, making Khan jump.

60

"Steady, girl," I murmured, my high spirits sagging again. Being nice to Sarah was like being nice to a piranha. *God, why did Sarah have to be part of the deal?*

Farley was laughing and Ian was pointing to his throat, making gagging sounds.

"What gives here?" asked Dad.

"Obviously you don't know Sarah," said Ian drily.

"I've seen her."

"When Emily and Sarah were in eighth grade," said Ian, "I picked Em up at school one day. I drove up just in time to see Sarah launch something at Emily."

"A milk carton," I said. "Full."

"What did you do?" asked Farley.

"I dodged and then threw it back."

Ian said, "As I recall, Emily was a better shot.

"I bet that improved your relationship," said Dad.

"Yeah. Sarah didn't come near me for two weeks."

"Really, Emily. You're growing up now. Can't you at least be courteous to the girl?"

I rubbed Khan's neck under her mane, and she leaned into my hand. "Sarah's hard to be polite to."

"I'm ashamed that Mr. Petersen has to ask you to be nice to his daughter. Especially after all Sarah's been through with her mother."

Sarah's mother had killed herself five or six years ago. It was a big scandel, because the Petersens are well known in the horse industry. Sarah never said a word about it, but the news reports said Sarah had been the one to find her mom.

Dad wasn't through. "You have every reason to be kind to her. Not to mention that it's Christlike."

That stung. I chomped at my retainer.

"Sarah would drop dead if Emily were nice to her," said Ian.

"I doubt it. I want you to be friendly with this girl,

61

Emily. Why don't you invite her to church?"

Sarah would laugh her head off if I invited her to church. I sighed. How could something so good suddenly turn into something so awful?

"Well, Emily?"

"I'll try," I said, forcing the words out.

"Farley, get down from there now," said Dad. "You and Ian run along to the house. Emily and I will be there in a minute."

Khan nosed my arm. Dad leaned back against the wooden manger, crossing his arms over his chest. I braced myself for more sermon about Sarah.

"Are you sure you want to buy that horse?" he asked. I nodded, staring at his scuffed boots. "You could buy another horse with that money."

"I know," I said. "But I want Khan."

"Okay." He straightened up and got busy cleaning her wounds, feeling her legs for hidden injuries.

I held Khan. She was mine—or would be after tomorrow. I combed her untidy forelock with my fingers and braided it between her dark eyes.

Dad taped up her sore leg with cotton and wrapping. He said, "My first horse was an ugly chestnut. I bought him when I was about twelve. Money my grandparents had given me." He finished wrapping her leg and patted her rump gently. "There's something special about the first horse."

I didn't know what to say, except I was glad he was letting me buy her.

"I'll come in the house in a minute," I said. He nodded and picked up the bucket. I heard him put Bottom in another stall down the aisle. Slowly I pulled Khan's halter off. "Have you eaten?" I asked her. She lowered her head, sniffing the deep straw, the walls, and the horse next door. Finally she sniffed me. I held out my palms and she licked at them.

I handed her a flake of hay and she picked at it, not hungry. "You can't be homesick," I said. "Because you're home now."

She turned her back to me, her nose to the corner of the stall. Her flanks heaved. She looked very tired.

I stood quietly, just watching, marveling that she was mine. I prayed a lot, too.

Farley came to fetch me. When we left, Khan didn't even turn around.

Sleep well, Khan.

She shone like silver in the darkness of the stall.

7
Drinker of the Wind

The next day was Friday, the last day before spring vacation. During algebra, Mr. Hart passed back our tests, silently moving through the aisles, his thin face grim. Melissa got her test back first and gave me a satisfied grin. Then Mr. Hart handed me mine without a change in expression.

My fingers were cold as I took the paper. An "A." What a relief.

The class was quiet except for papers rustling as kids opened their tests. Across the room Sarah peeked at hers and shoved it into a folder. The florescent lights glimmered against her eyes; then she saw me and glared.

Be nice to her? No way. I clicked my retainer until the girl next to me said, "Gross, Emily."

Having passed out the remaining tests, Mr. Hart leaned against the blackboard tray. He had a perpetual white chalk slash across the seat of his slacks.

"Class," he said, rubbing the bridge of his nose under his plastic frame glasses. "I'm not happy with your test scores. Only seven of you got an A, B or C. The rest of you got D's and F's. What's the problem?

We've gone over these sections for some time now."

Everyone murmured. I glanced down at my A and felt guilty. Ian had helped me, and I had taken pre-algebra in junior high, so I was better off than most of the kids.

Melissa leaned back in her seat and lifted the edge of her test. C + .

"All right," I said under my breath. I showed her my test score, and we grinned at each other.

Jason, Stallion's younger brother, raised his hand. I paid attention to him, not because I liked him, but because he was related to Stallion. "The work is hard," he said. His voice was deep and didn't crack like it had last year. "I mean, I do the homework and everything, but I don't understand it."

"Yeah," someone called out. "It makes sense in class; then at home it doesn't."

Mr. Hart nodded. "This is a big class, so I can't help you all individually, but I have an idea. Since spring break is starting—and for some of you it has already started," he added drily, directing his gaze toward a bunch of kids in the back, who immediately straightened up. "I'm going to pass out homework based on the last chapters. When we come back from vacation, we'll take the test again."

"What if we do worse the next time?" asked a brown-haired guy with a gold stud in his ear.

"I hope you'll do better. An F is as low as you can get." Laughter bounced off the walls. Mr. Hart pushed his glasses up. "I'll take the higher score if one of you does worse. But you shouldn't, if you do the homework." He handed out a blank sheet of paper to each row. "I want you all to pair up and meet with your partner at least three times. So I advise finding someone close to where you live. There are thirty-eight of you, so everyone will have a partner."

A girl with kinky red hair said, "I'm going to visit my grandmother in Wyoming."

"Get Granny to help you," yelled a guy from the back.

"So I know that you have met with your partner, you will write up a brief paragraph each time you meet. At least three sessions," said Mr. Hart.

More groans.

"Five minutes," said Mr. Hart, "and you match up with someone. I don't care if you both got F's." He began handing out ditto sheets.

The girl going to her grandmother's wasn't exempt. She had to find someone in Wyoming. She said, laughing, "There's a cute guy next door."

"Go for it," said Jason.

On the white sheet of paper being passed around, Melissa and I wrote our names together.

"I wish I could write Ian's name down," she whispered.

"What? And miss the opportunity to work with me?" Melissa stuck her tongue out at me.

Mr. Hart gathered up the papers with names on them. A few kids didn't have partners, so he matched them. The girl going to Wyoming made the class number odd, and Sarah was the one left over. And I snickered to myself. Sarah was odd.

"We need a threesome here," said Mr. Hart. "Who lives close to Sarah?"

I chomped on my retainer as Mr. Hart's gaze moved up and down the aisle. No one spoke up, and Sarah's voice cut through the thick silence. "It's okay. My dad or my cousin can help me."

"I'd rather it was someone from our class."

I busied myself looking through my notebook. The numbers on my homework closed in, suffocating my thoughts. My breath came almost in gasps. *Someone else can help her. I don't want to. . . .*

Jason's voice broke the tension. "Sarah can join Mark and me." He and Mark winked at each other, and Mr. Hart wrote down Sarah's name.

Sarah bit her lip, then Jason elbowed her and said something that made them both laugh. Looking up, smiling, her blonde hair flung back, she suddenly met my gaze and her face grew haughty. The princess was furious because I had the audacity to look at her. So I stared longer, until Jason bumped her and she broke the gaze. She would have laughed in my face if I'd offered to help.

"Let's get to work," said Mr. Hart. "Turn to page 227."

He scribbled on the blackboard and I took notes, but my thoughts stayed uncomfortably on Sarah.

After school Dad was waiting for me in the old Ford pick-up.

"How was school?" he asked as I slammed the door. He shifted gears and we rumbled away.

"Glad it's vacation."

At the credit union I withdrew five hundred dollars. I actually had five hundred and fifty-six dollars and ninety-seven cents, but I didn't want to give Mr. Petersen all my money. Back in the truck I sat quietly, holding the white envelope with its five one-hundred dollar bills. I'd never held so much money before. I knew I was buying Khan very cheap, but it still seemed like a lot of money.

As we drove closer to the Petersens', turning off Broken Hills Road and onto the road leading home, the truck seat squeaked. Dad said in a gentle voice, like he uses when he soothes colts, "Are you sure you want to buy Khan? You don't have to."

"Yes," I said fiercely, feeling hot and suffocated.

"I want to be sure they don't hurt her again. And I don't think Khan is the kind of horse Mr. Petersen thinks she is. Besides, I've never owned a horse all to myself."

Dad didn't respond. I knew he was thinking that I was buying Khan for the wrong reasons—at least in part. He turned off the road and up the gravel drive. Horses grazed in red clover pastures fenced in with white wooden boards.

"When I was a boy," said Dad, "I had a friend whose father had been stationed in Egypt where the real Arabian horses are. The desert bred. He said they were extremely intelligent, uncanny animals. Of course, the Bedouins treated them like equals and even let their war mares sleep in the family tents. The drinkers of the wind—that's what he called them." Dad smiled, and the corners of his eyes crinkled. "Perhaps Khan is a throwback to the drinkers of the wind."

"I hope so." Drinkers of the wind. I had heard of the Look of the Eagles, the fierce racing desire that good Thoroughbreds had that just spilled out of them and made their eyes glow. Khan had seemed like she ought to be out galloping, racing the sands, drinking in the wind. "I want to be friends with her," I said. "I think she needs a friend."

I had a deeper feeling, one that had images but not concrete words. Khan flying up the road out of the darkness, Khan in the shadows of the oak grove—I had rescued her twice. Why had it been me, and not another person? I thought I was meant to have her.

Dad parked the truck, and I slid out slowly. We headed for the main barn where Mr. Petersen's office was located.

The barn smelled fresh and airy, the sharp cedar scent dominant. Sleek horses in stalls pricked their ears at our approach. They had temperature control, automatic fly spray every half hour, thick bedding.

Dad raised his eyebrows. "Nice," he said, sounding like Ian. "Very nice."

I peered into one stall, and a steel gray stallion flared his nostrils. He stood fetlock deep in straw. The walls were padded with blue material. Amazing. The barn must have held fifty horses. I allowed myself the luxury of a wistful sigh.

Footsteps ticked toward us. Around the corner came Mr. Petersen, and behind him was Sarah. Dad jerked his chin at her, and I nodded.

"Well, young lady," boomed Mr. Petersen. "Ready to sign your life away?"

Dad gave me a trace of a smile and shook hands with Mr. Petersen. Sarah and I ignored each other.

"Office is upstairs," said Mr. Petersen. The spurs on his boots jangled down the aisle to a narrow staircase. Horses popped up to the stall doors, dished faces thrust out, watching us. I clung to Dad's side.

Mr. Petersen's office was like a treehouse, above the barn, enclosed in glass so he could observe each horse in its stall. He opened the door and let us in. Air conditioned. I could get used to this fast.

Sarah sprawled on the leather couch while Dad and I sat in straightback chairs in front of Mr. Petersen's huge, curved desk. Papers were strewn over the surface, reminding me of the messy cardtable Dad used to do his bookwork on.

Sarah sat silently, playing the bereft widow. I'd seen the same look on her face in eighth grade when another girl stole her boyfriend. The guy had dumped Sarah for a normal girl, and Sarah had moped for days.

"Here we are," said Mr. Petersen, handing us some papers. "Take your time reading them. It's change of ownership papers, pedigree, and the clause about Khan's first living foal."

He had never said anything about Khan's first foal being stillborn.

"Can I get you anything? Water? Coke?" He pointed to a small refrigerator. We shook our heads.

Dad read over my shoulder. The three pages took a long time to state that I was buying Khan for five hundred dollars and her first foal would be offered to Mr. Petersen. Attached was her pedigree. She had *Bask in her bloodlines, both top and bottom. The asterisk meant an imported horse. Also attached was her International Arabian Horse Association Registration.

Behind me Sarah was swinging her legs, *thunk*, *thunk*, into the leather couch. She chewed her gum loudly, snapping it, popping it, as she flipped through a magazine. I ignored her. If I said, "Dad, she's bothering me," he'd say, "She's just sitting there." Which was true, but it was the *way* she sat there.

After I'd signed my name about half a million times, I handed Mr. Petersen the envelope. He took the money out and laid the bills in a drawer. Sarah gave a great sniff. Crocodile tears.

"Really, Sarah," said Mr. Petersen. "That mare wasn't for you. I don't know where you got the notion that she was."

"I was going to retrain her," said Sarah, glaring hard at me.

"Retrain her?" I said. "That's hardly the word. Mistreat her is more like it."

Sarah threw the magazine against the couch. "I wanted to ride her in shows," she said.

"Buck up," said Dad briskly. "Horses are a business. You can't make pets out of them." How many times had I heard that lecture?

"Emily is," said Sarah in a wavery voice.

"Hardly," answered Dad. "The mare'll be a brood mare. Not a toy."

"I could have retrained her," said Sarah. She leapt to her feet, her tears dried up and her eyes blazing. "But Emily ruined that."

"It's not my fault that you don't know what you're doing," I snapped.

"Emily," said Dad. "Please. Girls, this is a business transaction. Let's leave the emotion out of it."

Sarah stomped for the door.

"Sarah, sit down," said her father.

"No!" She slammed the door so the windows trembled.

Mr. Petersen shook his head as Sarah stormed down the steps. She must have been practically jumping on the boards.

Dad had a light in his eyes. If I had done that, he would have knocked me into the next county.

"Teenagers," said Mr. Petersen with a tight smile.

Dad pursed his lips, and I could tell he was biting back his words.

Through the glass I watched Sarah lead her bay Thoroughbred out of its stall and take him outside. I took a deep breath. My heart was pounding. Dad and Mr. Petersen talked a moment more. I hugged the pedigree and owner's papers to my chest.

"Give me a call in a few weeks," said Mr. Petersen, "after she's gotten used to your place, and we'll see about breeding her."

I nodded.

As we started out the door, he added, "Remember what I said about the other condition on Khan?"

I met his gaze. Dad's eyes bored into me like talons. I nodded again. "I'll try."

"Sometimes I don't know what to do with that child."

Dad made a sympathetic noise.

"Can you folks find your way out?"

Dad assured him we could, and we filed down the stairs into the tidy barn and then outside where sunlight tumbled in and out of fog floating in from the north.

Dad got into the truck. As I stood waiting for him to unlock my door, hoofbeats came up behind me. Sarah sat on her Thoroughbred hunter and fixed her frosty blue eyes on me. In a flat and unemotional voice, not filled with fury or tears, she said, "I'll get you for this, Emily. Just you wait."

She spun the horse off his hocks and cantered away.

Dad unlocked the door, and I climbed in.

"What did she say?"

"Nothing much." Her cool voice conveyed more than all her bluff and fake tears. I was finally frightened, but I didn't want to admit it.

8
Stranger in
the Night

I carefully placed Khan's papers by my bed to look at them later. Then I changed my clothes and grabbed two apples, tucking one in my Levi vest and biting into the other.

The winds pushed the clouds around like sheepdogs after wayward lambs. When Ian and I were younger, we used to lie on our backs and make up stories about the clouds. Sometimes at night, when I'd had a bad dream and was too scared to cross the floor lest something grab me and drag me under the bed, Ian would somehow sense that and come in and sit on my bed. He'd tell me stories about clouds and chase away my bad dreams.

At the trainee barn, I stopped to see Khan in the stall down on the end. I hung over the pipe fencing. During the day the stalls were oepn, so the horses can come and go as they please into the paddocks.

Khan pointed her ears at me.

"Come here," I said and pulled the apple from my vest.

She didn't come closer. Sunlight splashed over her gray coat, dark as ocean mist. She'd lighten as she grew older. Her name and tail were translucent in the light.

"You're mine, Khan. Did you know that?" She didn't act too thrilled. What if we didn't become friends?

I stood with the apple in my palm for a while, watching Khan and watching the clouds shift. Finally I put the apple in her outside tub, for when we fed in the paddock, and got Cobol.

As I groomed him, he ran his lips over my hand and the dandy brush. "Silly," I said. He watched with bright eyes and pressed his mouth on my arm, his tongue wet and hot. I grabbed his tongue and gently pulled. He lifted his upper lip, a horse laugh.

Mounting him, I sent him into the hills, sweeping past the reservoir, just riding for pleasure. "Spring vacation," I said, and he cocked back an ear. "We can play for once."

Purplish flowers grew along the path that narrowed as it traveled into the hills. Cobol's muscles were glossy under his skin and he breezed along, cantering eagerly, hopping over imagined hurdles in the road. Suddenly he propped, head up, mane a black shiver in my face, all four legs stiff under him, and slid to a halt.

I was flung against his neck, the saddle horn jutting into my belly. I gasped, the air gone from my lungs, but steadied Cobol automatically, my hands low on his neck.

The colt stood rigid, his nostrils red and distended, and stared at a clump of oaks.

"More monsters?" I asked softly. He twitched his ear back, then strained forward as tiny crackles like a string of firecrackers came from the oaks.

Apprehension pooled in my stomach. Cobol shied as a horse and rider crunched out from behind the trees. Nigel again.

I didn't like his popping up everywhere. Cobol nickered, and the chestnut with splashy, white legs whickered back.

"Hello," said Nigel. He had a leather satchel tied to the cantle of his English saddle. He held the wide leather reins between the fingers of both hands.

"What are you doing here?" I blurted out.

A smile touched his eyes, then trickled down to his lips. I stared, fascinated. It was the first time I'd seen him look anything other than mad.

"Don't you believe in greetings?"

"Sorry. Hello. What are you doing here?"

He patted the satchel. "I collect flowers and plants."

"Why?"

He shrugged. "Because I'm interested in botony." He patted his horse's neck and added, "Although I usually hike. The horses tend to eat my best specimens."

I chuckled. The horse shook his head and snorted. He was tall, over sixteen hands, with brilliant white legs and a lightening slash down his muzzle. I wanted to ask if he'd been jumping that horse last night, but I didn't want to say I'd been spying from the hillside.

"Is that your horse?" I asked, figuring that was safe.

"Yes. I trained him from a baby. I've ridden him in some one-day events, but mostly he's a dressage horse."

Braggard. But I was envious. "I'd like to learn that stuff."

"Showing isn't all that it's cracked up to be. It's hard work."

He said it in a superior sort of way and I bristled. "Training colts isn't exactly easy."

He glanced at Cobol, standing, chewing at his bit. "I suppose not. Whenever I've seen you riding, you've been on those bouncy, green horses."

"When have you seen me riding?"

The wind tossed his hair. "In the hills. I've seen you and that little kid."

"My brother, Farley."

"He rides well for a kid."

I wasn't sure if that was a compliment or not. "I'll be sure to tell him you said so."

We were silent a moment. Cobol shifted his weight, chewing harder on the rollers, grinding them. Nigel sat very correct on his horse—unlike me. I sat with my legs far forward, nearly on the colt's shoulders, because I never knew when a colt would give a tremendous leap or buck, and I held on better that way. Nigel didn't look stiff or unnatural, but like he and the horse fit together. A centaur.

"What kind of horse is he?" I asked. "He looks like a Thoroughbred, sort of." I ran through breeds in my mind, discarding them.

"Pasha is Hanoverian," he said. I started to ask him how he got a German horse when he said, "I heard you bought Khan this afternoon."

I stiffened. "So?"

He slapped the ends of the reins against his thigh. "Sarah wanted to retrain Khan, to show her father that she could be useful. Her dad thinks of her as a beautiful object that doesn't do anything. It bothers Sarah, so I told her I'd help. We took Khan out into the hills, and that mare went crazy. That's when you rode up."

"So I'm the bad guy, huh?"

"Come on, Emily," he said, his accent thickening. "You and Sarah have had a grudge between you for a long time. Why is that? I can't get Sarah to tell me much. Did you have a big fight?"

I frowned. "We don't smell right to each other."

"What?" He gave me a funny look.

"We instinctively don't like each other. I can't really explain it, except we do everything in opposite ways."

Nigel rubbed his chin. "Look, Emily, I don't know how you'll take this—and I'm not sure if I know myself what I mean—but I admire you. I don't know you well, but I like what I know of you. And I'd like to know you better." He looked me full in the face; my heart started pounding. "But I also care for Sarah." He slapped the ends of the reins some more.

I remembered my conversation with Melissa—either Nigel is nice and Sarah's nice, or Nigel isn't nice and Sarah's not, either. I shook my head. "Is Sarah your girlfriend?"

Nigel laughed. It was more shocking than his anger or his refusal to speak. "My girlfriend?" He laughed again.

"What's so funny?"

"Sarah's my cousin. That's why I keep Pasha there. I work for my uncle, Sarah's dad. My mom and I live about a mile away."

Cousins. I felt like a foolish colt. "So that explains why you're friendly with her."

The laughter fell from his face. "Sarah has been a good friend to me during . . . during a difficult time in my life. If she weren't my cousin, we'd still be friends."

He turned his horse around. "I'm glad you have Khan," he said. "Sarah was a little rough with her. I always felt there was something good in Khan, although none of us seemed to be able to find it."

He sent the horse into a trot. Amazing. I didn't even see the cues. I stared as the horse cantered and cleared a fallen branch, his tail flickering up like a question mark. He landed, and Nigel looked back as if he knew I'd be watching.

My face burned, but I had to laugh at myself for gawking. Flower collector. Good rider. All of a sudden I had a feeling that Nigel had been waiting for me, and unease crawled over me. How often had he seen me? I never noticed him.

I rode Cobol home and he was quiet, pacing along the path. After dinner, I finished chores. Dad had warned me that Khan better not keep me from work. But when I was done, I hurried across the dirt to her stall. The night breathed cold and swept up through my feet. When I reached Khan's stall, Farley was sitting on the door and Khan was snuffling in her manger.

"Dad'll kill you if he sees you up there."

He jumped down. "Dad's on the phone with Megan. He doesn't notice much then."

Megan went to our church—taught Farley's Sunday school class, actually. It was nice to see Dad showing interest in someone, but we all felt a little funny about it.

I unlatched the door, and we walked in. Khan lifted her face, alfalfa flowers in her forelock. She rested her weight on her off back leg, and it didn't seem to pain her.

I set my algebra book and homework on the corner of her manger. She sniffed at the book and snorted. "My sentiments, exactly," I told her.

"Khan and I have been talking," said Farley.

"What about?" I checked the outside tub. She had eaten the apple.

"Philosophic viewpoints."

I laughed. "And what is Khan's philosophy?"

The mare licked at the inside of her manger. Farley said, "She believes good will ultimately come one day. She hopes humans aren't all as bad as the ones she's encountered."

I hope you're right, Khan, I thought to her. I sat down in the shavings, leaning against the wooden slats. Farley sank down beside me. Khan sniffed at me, drooling green over my hands. "Thanks," I said and wiped my fingers on my jeans.

She returned to her manger, and I opened my algebra book.

"Why are you doing your homework out here?"

"So Khan gets used to having me around."

He snuggled against my shoulder, yawning. "Is Sarah going to beat you up?"

"She'd better not."

"Sarah is a dead planet," he said. "Nothing wants to live there."

Except Nigel. He saw good in her. "Really, Farley," I said. "I can hardly write with you like a puppy against me."

He moved a fraction of an inch. Khan dozed, occasionally swishing her tail. Farley watched me trying to answer the problem of x. I erased a lot.

"How can a letter be a number?"

"It just is."

"How stupid. Letters aren't numbers."

"It's a metaphor."

"It's dumb."

"I guess you have to be a grownup to understand."

He gave me a look that said, "Don't pull rank on me." Then, sounding innocent, which he wasn't, he said, "You mean algebra is like sex?"

"What an interesting theory, Farley," said Melissa, hooking her arms over the stall door.

I grinned up at her. "Come on in. Khan shouldn't mind."

She unlatched the door. "So this is the famous Khan."

The mare stopped chewing and stared at Melissa. When Melissa put out her hand, Khan politely sniffed it, then went back to hunting missed stalks of hay.

"She doesn't act wild and uncontrollable."

"Why should she? I'm not beating her."

We laughed. Melissa sat next to me and kicked Farley's shoe playfully. He kicked back with a grin.

"You want to hear something weird?" I asked.

"Sure. I'm into weird."

I told her about Nigel and our conversation. I didn't tell her about Nigel wanting to get to know me better, because I was afraid she'd tease me.

"So he's Sarah's cousin," Melissa said. "Interesting."

"So what does it mean, Doctor?"

"Serious. I think we need to operate."

"I'll say. Frontal lobotomy."

We giggled. Khan extended her neck, sniffing at my shoes. I pulled a carrot out of my vest pocket. She sniffed at it warily, as if she hadn't seen a carrot before. Finally she pulled it from my fingers, dropped it on the shavings, and crunched it. She drooled orange foam.

"Slobbery thing," said Melissa.

"But she's beautiful." And she was. Silvery-gray like Christmas tree tinsel. Wide, gazelle eyes. A tingly feeling pierced me. She was mine.

"What are you going to do with her?"

"Ride her. Get foals from her. I've been reading some of Dad's books again, and there's this guy who trains horses without a bridle or saddle. It's training without fear."

"Without fear? Not for the rider!"

"No. I'll ride Khan in the bull pen so she can't go too crazy. Mostly I want her to know I'm her friend."

Melissa nodded. "She knows that already."

"I hope so."

Farley laid his head in my lap and breathed deep and even. Melissa and I did some of the homework assignments, but we knew a lot of it already.

As we finished a set of problems, I glanced at my watch. Ten-fifteen. No wonder Farley had conked out. Funny Dad hadn't come looking for us. Maybe he was still talking to Megan on the phone. And grownups said kids talked on the phone too much. . . . I shut my book and leaned my head against the wood slats. Then I heard footsteps outside in the aisle.

"Dad?" I called. The footseps halted, but no answer came. Melissa and I looked at each other.

"Who's there?" I called louder. Sliding Farley off my lap—he didn't wake up—I looked out of the stall.

"Ian?" Melissa said.

Khan looked over our heads, curling her nostrils and flattening her ears to her skull. Then she retreated to the far end of the stall, carefully moving around Farley's sleeping form.

We walked out into the aisle. Cool air struck. Moist hills. Shadows clung beyond the barn lights, and the moon's belly hung between clouds, a sleepy beacon.

I searched the darkness, trying to see the maker of the footsteps. Across the drainage ditch was land that ran wild with weeds and the small sheep pasture. The wind tossed the mustard and wild radish plants. Then I saw a movement. Melissa grabbed my hand.

Behind us Khan let out a rolling snort. Nothing moved except the breeze-tossed plants. I'm not sure how long Melissa and I stood, holding hands, staring into the darkness, but my eyes burned from not blinking.

Muffled sounds of horse hooves in the grass came across the pasture.

"I've gotta find out who that is," I hissed.

"Emily," began Melissa.

"Stay here and watch Khan and Farley. I'll be right back."

I ran across the dirt and leaped the drainage ditch,

blindly, and landed in a mustard bush. The horses' hooves quickened.

If only the moon were brighter. I crested a hill, panting, and the hooves drummed. Through the veil of the night, I saw a blur of a horse—no, two horses. Galloping now, heading for the reservoir. In the pale light I saw that one of the horses had white, white legs.

9
Breathless Canter

Saturday morning I walked through the sheep pasture, looking for evidence left by whoever had been here last night. I was sure it was Nigel and Sarah.

Fresh hoofprints were cut into the ground, and the grass along the fences was trampled. I followed the hoofprints to the back gate of the sheep pasture. It was open. Good thing we hadn't had any horses out in the pasture. I squatted, putting my fingers in the slices of prints. Shod horses. That was all I could tell. They were common looking prints.

I shut the back gate and retraced my steps. When I got to the barn, Dad was looking in at Khan.

"Last night two riders came up to our barn," I told him. "When I called out, they took off."

His eyebrows knit together. "Did you see who they were?"

I clicked my retainer. "I recognized Nigel's horse."

"You'll have to do better than that."

"Well, even if it wasn't them, there was someone around. Melissa saw, too."

Dad pushed back his visor. "You don't accuse someone unless you know for sure."

"Forget it." I leaned on the stall door. What if Sarah tried to sneak in and steal Khan? Maybe I ought to sleep in the barn.

Dad took down Khan's halter. "Let's longe her. I suspect she's favoring her leg more from stiffness than a real injury. She's a tough mare."

Even if Dad didn't think the riders last night were a threat, I hoped I'd see Nigel again. Maybe I could match up his horse's hooves with the prints. Plaster of Paris would freeze the horse print—not that I had any, of course.

We led Khan up to the riding arena and snapped on the blue longe line. Dad sat on the fence as I shook out the line.

"Walk," I commanded Khan. She circled, her tail clenched right, her ears half back. She walked several times around me, the line hanging between us, an umbilical cord. "Reverse." She stopped, pivoted toward me and walked the other direction, never relaxing her tail, walking tense as if she expected something bad to happen.

"Someone's trained her to longe," I said.

"Tell her to trot," called Dad.

I did. Khan flattened her ears, but broke into a shuffling trot. I clucked to her, but she refused to move out. "Some race horse," I said.

I reversed her. She wasn't limping, but she wasn't moving freely either.

"Whoa." She halted and faced me.

"I'll be right back," said Dad and he vaulted over the fence.

I walked up to Khan, folding the tape. At thoroughbred farms, the trainers taught the babies to longe, so I wasn't surprised that Khan knew how. "How come you don't like to longe?" I asked her. "Did someone mistreat you at the track?"

As I petted her and told her how beautiful she was, she arched her neck under my hand and unclamped her tail. I ran my hand down her off hind leg. It felt cool and hard, not feverish or puffy.

Dad appeared and climbed over the fence, holding a driving whip. "You don't need to hit her," he said, crossing the dirt towards us. "Just show it to her."

Khan saw him. Her ears flew back and she rocketed backward. I grabbed the line, but she reared straight up, jerking my feet from the ground for an instant before I let go. Staggering back, I tripped and landed on my bottom.

Khan reared higher, towering against the sky. Her heat suffocated me and her hooves dangled over my head, solid and black. I scrambled out of the way and grabbed at the line.

Savagely shaking her head, Khan yanked the line away from me, burning my palms, and bolted.

Dad grabbed for the blue line snaking by, but missed, and Khan galloped across the arena, the line reeling out behind her.

"I'm sorry, Emily." He flung the whip against the fence. "Even with those whip marks on her, I didn't expect such a violent reaction."

"At least she's not lame," I said wryly.

Khan stood in a corner, the longe line brilliant blue in the dust at her feet. I walked toward her, murmuring softly. When I was about thirty feet away, she shook her head. As I reached for the line, she bolted again, kicking up the dust into columns of smoke.

"Khan!" The fence turned her, slowing her, and she trotted, beautifully extended, holding her head sideways, keeping the line from under her feet.

"Why do I have this feeling you've done this before?"

The brat. But at least I knew she had a gorgeous

trot. I looked back at Dad and he was shaking is head, pushing back his visor.

Khan halted, and I approached her again. "Listen, you snip. You better stand still or I'll send you off to auction for the dog food companies." She appeared unmoved by my insults, but she did allow me to pick up the end of the line, watching and blowing air out of her nose in a snort. I began folding the long line, explaining to her that I really wanted to be friends and that we'd never show the whip to her again.

She pointed her ears at me. Finally I tugged at the line and she came, her quivering nostrils showing their red lining.

I led her back to Dad, and she rolled her eyes at him.

"It's all right, little girl," said Dad and slowly held up his arms. "I haven't got the whip. No more whips."

She stared at him for a long moment, snorted, and dropped her face, rubbing her check against her leg.

Longeing her again, I asked her to trot. She extended better, but when she cantered, she tucked her tail during the first circle. The second time around, her head came up and her tail curved over her hocks, a silver sweep. She reached mightily, her muscles singing under her smooth skin, each hoof striking the ground in a perfect, even tempo. The wind caught her mane and tail, silvering them. She thrust up her head, her pink rimmed nostrils open wide, sucking in the air as she cantered, floated, soared over the ground, a breath of the desert—a drinker of the wind.

She cantered around me several more circuits; then, dazed, I slowed her. Khan stopped, faced me, her flanks rising and falling, a thin sheet of sweat on her shoulders. "Good, good, girl," I said. She put her ears forward, listening to me.

"You did fine, Em," said Dad.

"You did fine, Khan," I echoed softly. She shook back her mane and yawned, showering me with wet dots of sweat.

After I cooled Khan off, I put her in the sheep pasture with Bottom, who was delighted and kept sniffing her and prancing around stiff legged, his knee popping. But he seemed to have a settling effect on Khan, even though he was excited.

The rest of the day I rode Io and a new filly to me, Ariel. I had named her. I wanted something pretty, after Ian's computer and outer space names.

Between horses, I stopped and sat on the fence post, watching Khan graze in the sun, her teeth clicking along the grass shoots. Every once in a while, she'd turn and rest her head on Bottom's broad rump, her eyes half closed.

"Good girl," I said. "You're a good girl." Her eyes flickered, then she dropped her head back to graze.

Dad walked by with a dark bay filly, heading for the bull pen. "Don't forget that Megan's coming for dinner," he called.

"I remember." How could I have forgotten that? Oh, well. She was nice enough. I put Khan back in the barn and started my chores.

10
The Dinner Event

I hurried into the house to shower and change for dinner. I pulled on a skirt and blouse and brushed my hair in front of the mirror. If I were a horse, I'd be a regular bay color. I looked better with mascara, but I didn't feel like getting "gussied up," as Dad would say. Not for Megan.

I tucked in my blouse and padded barefoot out to the kitchen. The radio was blarring country twang music, and Dad and Ian were fussing around like two old hens. Farley sat at the table playing with plastic figures of He-Man and Battle Cat, who was yowling loudly in time with the music.

"I'm going to get Megan," said Dad. "Watch the coals, Ian."

"Okay." Ian was laying down the place settings around Farley.

The front door slammed shut.

"Doesn't Megan have a car?" asked Farley.

"He's being nice and picking her up," I said, reaching for some carrots to wash.

Ian fiddled with the radio tuner until a rock station erupted.

"Hey, Battle Cat likes the song that was playing."

"Tough toenails," said Ian.

I sliced carrots in time to the fast beat. "Party down," I said.

"Yeah," said Ian. "So we're going to officially meet Megan."

I frowned and dumped the carrots into a smoked glass serving dish. "What's that supposed to mean? Megan's been at church for ninety million years."

"At least that long," said Farley. Battle Cat leaped gracefully over a plate.

"It means that I think Megan is becoming Dad's girlfriend," said Ian, sitting in the chair across from Farley, his leg over the chair arm.

"Well, she's a friend, I guess, and a girl, sort of—actually she's too old to be a girl, anymore—so I guess that makes her a girlfriend."

Ian wrinkled his nose as Farley jumped Battle Cat in front of his face. "Don't, Farley."

"He's got to practice."

"Practice somewhere else."

I sliced cucumbers and tomatoes and tore up leaves of romaine lettuce. I thought I'd grate cheese on top and cut up olives, too. Dad was going to barbecue shish kebabs when he returned. "Don't forget about the coals, meathead," I said to Ian.

"Don't worry. They're under control."

"Does Dad kiss Megan?" asked Farley. He had the same look on his face as he did the time he slipped and fell on a banana slug.

"Who cares?" I said, throwing the ends of the tomatoes into the sink. But I did care. I cared terribly.

"I think Dad's lonely," said Ian.

"Why?" asked Farley. "He has us."

"We don't keep him warm on a cold night," said Ian, sounding like an expert.

"David got into trouble for going to bed with his girlfriend," announced Farley. Battle Cat made a tremendous leap over the salt and pepper shakers.

"David who?" asked Ian.

"King David. In the Bible. You're supposed to wait until you get married, right?"

"What would you think if Dad got remarried?" asked Ian.

I had thought about that before. "I don't want another mother. Maybe if she were nice, it would be all right."

"Megan's nice."

"Do you know something we don't?" I demanded, slamming down the paring knife.

Farley stared at Ian, his mouth open, Battle Cat in his hand.

Ian glanced at us both briefly. "It's just that Dad is really interested in Megan, that's all."

"If Dad got married again," said Farley, "we wouldn't have to cook or clean."

"Don't be so sure," said Ian, swinging his leg. "Women's lib and all. She'd know a good deal when she saw one."

I tore up leaves of the lettuce. Images of Dad and Megan surfaced in my mind, of them kissing, eating breakfast, watering the garden, petting the horses. Was Dad lonely? He was so busy, how could he have time to be lonely? Maybe he kept busy so as *not* to be lonely. He and Mom had been divorced almost two years now. A lifetime ago.

"You'd have to give up your room," I said.

"Forget it," said Farley. "She can live in the barn."

"I won't live at home forever," said Ian. "I still want to transfer to Cal Tech."

"I don't believe I'll ever get married," said Farley. "It's too much trouble."

"That's what Paul says," I said.

"Paul who?" asked Ian.

"The apostle Paul."

We all started laughing. Hysterically, I think.

"David who?" yelled Farley.

Ian said, "Paul who? David who?"

The front door opened. We tried to stop laughing, but every time I looked over at Ian, or Farley at me, we'd giggle.

Dad and Megan walked into the kitchen.

"What are you kids doing?" asked Dad, suspiciously.

"Getting dinner," said Ian.

Dad snorted and switched the radio back to country music.

"Looks like a great salad," said Megan, smiling and coming closer.

My lips twitched into a sort of smile. "Thanks," I said.

Megan was my Sunday school teacher last year. She was friendly enough, but I was as prickly as a hedgehog because I had just become a Christian. Everyone knew the rules except me. I didn't know the songs and couldn't look up a Bible verse without using the table of contents. But Melissa helped me, and after awhile I began to feel at home.

"I think you all know each other, right?" said Dad.

I stared at him, fascinated. His eyes were bright. He stood slim and tall in tan cords and a long sleeved brown-and-rust shirt. He looked handsome.

Ian grinned. "Hi, Megan."

"My oldest son, Ian. Farley, my youngest, and my daughter, Emily."

"Emily the weirdo," said Farley. I glared at him.

"Emily was in my class last year," said Megan, ignoring Farley's comment. She looked younger than

Dad. Her dress was neat and crisp, but casual. I felt frumpy. "I remember Emily did well memorizing verses."

My face grew hot. I had hated standing up and saying verses with all those eyes on me.

"I'll start the shish kebabs," said Dad, still giving us you'd-better-behave-or-else looks.

Megan helped him carry out the platters of meat, mushrooms, green peppers, cherry tomatoes, and pineapple that Dad had skewered together earlier.

I finished the salad. Ian switched the radio back to rock, and Farley played listlessly with He-Man and Battle Cat. The laughter had fled.

The beat of the music pounded my brain. Love, love, love, screamed the words. Why were all the songs on the radio about love? Lost love. Cheating love. Lying love. Yuck. Too much love.

What is love, really? It's evasive, like a wild colt —that's how it seems to me. Maybe you have to tame love. At church everyone, even Megan, says, "God is love." But if God is love, then why is love so weird and confusing?

Dad yelled from the backyard. "Is the salad ready?"

"Yes," I called.

"Table set?"

"Yes."

He came in with the shish kebabs. We had pulled up an extra chair for Megan, and she sat on Dad's right. I sat across from Megan between Farley and Ian.

"Would you like to say grace, Farley?" asked Dad, but Farley shook his head no. I kicked him under the table. He didn't kick back, but he glared sideways at me, looking a little white around his mouth and eyes.

"I'll say it, then." Dad and Megan held hands.

I clenched my hands in my lap. My eyes felt hot against my eyelids. After the grace, we all said

"Amen" except Farley, whom I kicked again. This time he kicked me back.

Dad and Megan talked together, with Ian chiming in cheerfully. I silently unspeared shish kebabs and piled up salad.

Megan said something; then there was silence.

I looked up and saw everyone looking at me. "Pardon?"

Dad gave me a small annoyed look.

"Your father says you have a new horse," Megan repeated. She did have pretty eyes. Bluish-gray.

"Khan's a Polish Arabian. I'm retraining her."

Megan smiled at me. "I grew up in the big city, so the only horses I saw were on television. I don't know much about them."

"Oh, we can teach you," said Ian.

He was terribly friendly. I couldn't tell if it was genuine or diplomatic.

"Do you have any kids?" asked Farley.

I hid my smile, but Megan didn't even try to stifle hers. Did the woman know how *not* to smile?

"I've never been married. But I've taught children for many years."

"How come you never got married?" Farley asked.

Ian and I exchanged strangled looks. I was just waiting for Farley to ask, *Do you and my dad kiss?* I coughed to cover up a laugh.

"That's enough, Farley," said Dad sharply.

"It's all right, John," said Megan. She fixed her gaze on Farley, who was pushing a tomato around on his plate. "I just never found the man I wanted to marry. Besides, if I had gotten married I probably couldn't have taught children in Africa as I did for six years." She broke off and said quickly, "Farley, are you all right?"

We stared at him. His face was white and his eyes

93

were like holes burned in his head. Suddenly he leaped up and ran out of the room.

I ran after him and found him in the hall bathroom, hanging over the toilet bowl. I shut the door and went to him, holding his head in my hands.

"Why didn't you say you didn't feel well?" I murmured.

The bathroom door opened and Dad, with Megan and Ian, crowded in. I flushed the toilet.

"Gross," said Ian.

"Shut up," croaked Farley. He leaned against me, looking like a very little boy.

"Flu, maybe?" said Dad.

Megan wet a washcloth and handed it to me, her eyes concerned. I wiped Farley's face and wished Megan would go away. She didn't belong.

"Let's get in bed, son," said Dad. He helped Farley change his clothes while I hovered in the hall with Megan and Ian.

"Poor little guy," she said.

"I'm not sleeping with him," said Ian. "I've got a big test coming up. I can't get sick."

"So go sleep in the barn," I said. I remembered what Farley had said about a new wife of Dad's sleeping in the barn because Farley wouldn't give up his room, but it wasn't funny now.

Dad came out of the boys' room, and I went in. The others went back to the kitchen. I put my hand on Farley's forehead. "You think you'll be sick again?"

"I hope not. I didn't mean to do it at dinner. But I'm sort of glad I did."

I stared. "Why?"

His eyes closed and fluttered open again. "I don't want Dad to get married again." His voice was soft and curiously detached. "What if I get to like her, and she leaves like Mom did?"

94

Tears sprang to my eyes. I didn't know what to say, but Farley didn't seem to want an answer. I sat next to him on the bed, not touching him, but watching him slip off to sleep.

Finally I said quietly, "I won't ever leave you, Farley." But even as I spoke a deep pang struck me. I couldn't keep that promise. No person could.

11
Friends

I woke Sunday as the sky paled pink like the smooth curve of a shell. My bedroom window faced east, but I couldn't yet see the sun. Early light shone through the lacy curtains. I snuggled under the comforter and closed my eyes, but the light urged me to rise.

Stepping over Ian, who was sprawled on my floor, wrapped in a blanket—true to his word not to sleep with Farley—I stripped off my nightgown and pulled on jeans and a sweater. Then I peeked in on Farley. He, too, was sound asleep, tangled in the sheets, his arm hanging over the bed.

I slipped outside.

Dawn steathily pushed back the night, but the pungent scent of the dark still hung in the air, along with strings of lingering fog. Horses nickered to me, and Cobol gave a tiny whinny. They knew it wasn't feeding time yet. I called Khan's name and looked in her stall, my shoulder bumping shut the door. *Bumping shut the door!* My stomach suddenly turned to ice: Khan's stall was empty.

I pounded out of the barn, heading for the gate that led to the hills—the *open* gate. Dad and I always latched that gate at night. I ran faster, my legs protesting, feeling like metal.

Sarah. She had come back and let Khan out or, worse, had taken her. I raced for the reservoir, figuring that if Khan were on her own, she would have headed for the hills.

Tears of anger filled my eyes. I'd kill Sarah.

My breath pierced me and I slowed, jogging up the hill. I should have grabbed Bottom, but now I didn't want to go back for him. I fingered my belt. If I found Khan, I could put the belt around her neck.

Cresting the hill, I saw only the flat, narrow valley and the reservoir, smooth and goldish from the sun. I jogged along the trail, searching in the shadows. Around a curve in a cluster of oaks was a band of animals. Mule deer, their large ears scooped toward me. Three white-flecked fawns stood with the band. A gray deer stood off to one side. A gray deer? No, it was Khan! *Thanks, God.* Khan stared out from among the deer. *Arabians are fleeter than gazelles.* I had read that once. It seemed proper that Khan had sought refuge with the deer.

Slowly the deer began to drift away over the hill, the fawns first, then the older deer, sleek and brown like rich loam. They moved away, gliding through the grass. Khan looked after them, her nostrils quivering.

I came closer, and she jerked her head up. The last deer vanished. Suddenly I heard a thin mewing and a fawn popped up. Both Khan and I jumped. The baby mewed again. Khan put out her nose, but the baby shied on spindly legs.

"Someone forget you?" I asked softly.

It ran in zig zag lines, mewing. A brown deer appeared from over the hill, and the fawn galloped, bleating, toward it. When it reached its mother, it thrust its head under her flank. The doe gazed at Khan and me with dark eyes, as if to say, "Thanks for not hurting my baby." With the fawn clinging to her side, they vanished.

Khan snorted.

"So," I said. "Who let you out?" She was going to have to come to me, because I could hardly chase her. A verse from the Old Testament came to mind, "If you have run with footmen and they have tired you out, then how can you compete with horses?" I couldn't.

I crouched down in the grass. Khan dropped her head and grazed. I could get Dad to rope her, but I wanted her to let me catch her. She had had enough people forcing her to obey.

The grass soaked my tennis shoes. The sun loomed up, shimmering in the fog.

Khan grazed closer. I played with my retainer, thinking.

Should I talk to Mr. Petersen and tell him about his daughter?

Remember what Dad said. You don't have proof.

But who else would do this? I know I latched the stall door and I know Dad latched the pasture gate.

Doesn't matter. You didn't actually see her. You need proof.

I could talk to Nigel. Would he know anything? But I'm sure I saw his horse Friday night. Maybe I'll start sleeping in the barn. I'll borrow Ian's camera and catch Sarah in the act.

Khan grazed in a half circle before me, her teeth clicking the new shoots, pretending nonchalance. The sun spilled over the hills. "I have to get back to watch Farley while the others go to church," I said and slowly stood.

Khan blew air loudly, raising her head.

I held out my hand for so long that I thought she had gone into a trance. My lower back ached. Then she extended her muzzle, barely brushing my fingertips. Stepping closer, she breathed air at my face. I blew back. She blew harder and then stopped, ears forward, expectant. I pulled my belt out of the loops, buckled it around her neck, and tugged.

She followed, swishing her tail. The sun rose higher and I was dazzled—not by sunlight, but by the joy inside that burned brighter and stronger than any sunlight I could see.

Khan and I were friends.

I turned Khan and Bottom out into the sheep pasture. I could see them, the silvery mare and the buttery gelding, from Farley's bedroom window, if I craned my neck.

I read aloud to Farley as he drifted in and out of sleep. When I stopped reading he didn't protest.

When the truck rattled up, I ran down to open the front door for Dad and Ian, home from church.

"How is the patient?" asked Dad, loosening his tie.

"Asleep."

"That's good. Poor kid. He looked terrible last night." Dad opened the refrigerator.

Ian came to the kitchen counter and leaned his elbows on the tile. The light from the small window smoothed over him, and suddenly Ian looked so much like Dad. The same glossy dark hair, the same brown eyes, the same way he held his head.

Unbuttoning his shirt cuffs, Ian glared, breaking the spell. "What are you staring at?"

"I don't know. I'm still trying to figure it out."

"Ha, ha." Ian yanked off his necktie and draped it over the back of a chair.

Dad took out lunch meat and cheese and began to make sandwiches.

"Cobol's owners are coming for him, either today or

tomorrow," said Dad. "I'll need you to polish him up."

I sat in a chair, watching him spread mayonnaise on bread, realizing I hadn't even eaten breakfast, but I didn't feel hungry. "I'll miss Cobol. He's a good colt."

Dad opened his mouth as if he was going to start in about, "Horses are a business; you can't treat them as pets." Instead he looked at me and said, "You've done a good job with him, Em. He'll always remember that and be a safe horse."

Cobol leaving. Why do things have to change? But they do, always. Thinking of Cobol reminded me of Khan and how she was out this morning. There was one thing that would never change—Sarah.

I didn't tell Dad about Khan being out, because he would think I had left the latch loose. Sometimes the stall doors warp and are hard to shut tightly, but I knew I didn't leave it unlatched. But, since I hadn't seen Sarah or anyone else, Dad would consider the case closed. No proof.

The phone rang. Ian answered it and came back grinning.

"For you, Em. It's a boy." He and Dad elbowed each other like kids.

"You two are disgusting," I said. I went to the phone, wondering who it was. "Hello, this is Emily."

"Emily, this is Nigel Waters. How are you?"

"Fine. What is it?" I was trying not to get mad. Maybe he didn't know what Sarah was doing, but he certainly had poor timing.

"My uncle suggested I call and ask if you wanted to see the stallions. There are a couple who would be compatible with Khan's bloodlines."

I twisted the phone cord. Dad and Ian were craning their heads, gawking at me. I turned my back to them, and they laughed like hyenas. "I guess so. I hadn't thought about it."

"How about this afternoon?"

"I have to do some work, but after that."

"I'll be at the covered arena," he said. "You can ask anyone where I am, and they'll know."

Big shot, I thought as we hung up.

Farley came out to the living room, wobbly, his hair messed up, rubbing his eyes. "Who was that?" he asked.

"Nigel."

"He was once a star," said Farley.

"How do you know that?"

Farley curled up in a chair, his eyes tired but not feverish. "Everyone is made up from recyled star stuff." He held out his hand, his too-short pajama sleeve exposing his flat wrist. "Our bodies are made from the same stuff stars are, so when stars died a long time ago the stuff got made into us. So Nigel is a star."

I stretched my arms over my head. "I guess I'd better be nice to him, then."

Farley nodded solemnly.

Dad and Ian came in to watch the ball game. I fixed a sandwich for myself and soup for Farley, and then I walked out to the barn, watching the dickey birds hop off and on the horses' feeding tubs, snitching grain. Khan was still grazing, so I groomed Cobol. He wasn't especially dirty.

When I'd finished him, I led Khan out and put Cobol with Bottom. Khan followed lazily, her tail brushing her hocks. "Pretty girl, Khan," I said, as I began to groom her. At her name she laid back an ear, as if asking, *Yes?* I led her up across the lawn to the living room window where Dad, Ian, and Farley were watching the bluish television screen.

"Dad?"

He jumped up and came to the window. "What are you doing?"

"I'm going to take Khan to the bull pen, okay? I thought I'd sit on her today."

We had talked briefly about me riding her, trying out working her without a saddle and bridle.

"All right. I'll come out in a few minutes and check on you."

Fair enough. Horse breaking wasn't a joke. It was better to have someone handy in case of problems.

Farley called from the window, "Horses were once stars!"

I waved to him. Khan jumped, hitting the end of the rope, her hooves cutting prints into the soft garden dirt. I steadied her and led her to the bull pen. The gate creaked and Khan started again, but after she sniffed the door, she seemed satisfied it wouldn't come off the hinges and eat her alive. I unsnapped the lead line and let her proceed on her own into the pen.

The bull pen was round, with solid wooden sides that leaned out at such an angle that a rider on a horse who moved against the fence wouldn't be scraped off. The pen was small enough that a horse couldn't work up enough speed to get out of control. Dad always rode the unbroke colts here first.

Walking slowly around the walls, the dust covering her hooves, Khan sniffed the dirt thoroughly, probably smelling all the horses here before her. Satisfied, she collapsed her forelegs, grunting, and went down, rolling onto her back.

"Thanks, Khan. So much for grooming."

The mare rolled over once, twice, a third time. She lay still regarding me, her legs tucked under her like a foal. Then she scrambled up and shook like a wet dog, dust flying. I sneezed.

"Good heavens."

Khan and I looked up. Dad stood on the small platform above the pen.

"I see Khan's taking a dust bath."

I sneezed again. "Now I need a bath."

Khan stayed in the center of the pen. I figured I'd just sit on her, maybe walk her around. She was used to being ridden, but I wanted her to learn new with me.

I walked up to her. She sniffed my hands, but she watched me as though she knew something different was going to happen. I put my hands on her withers. Her skin twitched. In the back of my mind, a chant was rising, *Help, God. Help, God.*

Khan was sly, and I didn't figure she'd instantly buck. But I didn't know what might set her off.

"Just gotta try, huh?"

She shook her head, her halter jangling. Both hands on her withers, I hopped, throwing my right leg over her back, careful not to kick—she was taller than Cobol—and settled easy on her back. My legs curled naturally around her sides, and I sat straight. Khan's ears shot back, not in anger, but listening, wondering what was on the agenda.

"Good girl," I said, stroking her neck under her mane. My heart pounded, but I shoved my fear deep into a pocket of my mind, not letting it flow down into my body where Khan would sense it and become frightened, too. I sat, petting her, murmuring everything that came to mind: Bible verses, snatches of songs, absurd conversations about stars. She listened, furry, gray ears back.

"Okay, Khan, walk. I want you to walk." I shifted my weight slightly and squeezed her with my calves, and she moved smoothly, not like the green broke colts who couldn't hold a straight line because of the unfamiliar weight on their backs.

Resting my hands on her withers, I sat relaxed, my legs quiet around her. The air was still and heavy.

Khan pushed through it effortlessly. After a few circles, I reversed her by laying my palm against her neck and squeezing with my outside leg. She hesitated, slowing, her tail twitching, then she reversed smoothly and continued walking in the other direction.

"Good girl!"

We walked more. A chicken hawk swooped overhead and vanished. I halted Khan by setting my weight back and sitting down hard on her spine. She stopped. A squeeze of my legs and she walked again and, after a confused moment when she tossed her head, I turned her in circles and serpentines with my weight and my hand against her warm neck.

"Whoa." I sat hard on her spine and she stopped. I sat for a long moment telling her what a good girl she was.

"Gonna sit there forever?" Khan glanced up as Dad's shadow fell into the pen. He was smiling. "She looks good, Em. She's a smart mare."

I smoothed Khan's mane and then slid off her, letting her snuffle my hands. How soft she was. Lips black, rubbery, pulling at my fingers. A warm glow filled me.

"We're friends, aren't we?"

Khan pulled back, flies snapping from her, and collapsed at my feet and rolled. I had to jump out of the way of her hooves. At least horses didn't pretend feelings, like people. I laughed as Khan rolled again and again.

12
Wind Song

Later in the afternoon I walked down the road to the Petersen ranch. The wind muttered ancient spells in the trees and curled itself around my feet. I was resigned to seeing Sarah. Had Nigel told her I'd be coming? I hoped not.

The covered arena was cool and dark and rang with the thud of hooves. How many times had I sat in their grandstand, wishing I had a show horse? I couldn't count. I leaned on the rail and watched the riders and horses. I heard someone walk up next to me, and by the sudden scent of perfume, I knew it was Sarah.

She tapped a riding crop against her English boot top. She wore jodhpurs and a tight, sleeveless cotton shirt, and her blonde hair feathered out of a black riding helmet.

"What are you doing here?" she asked.

"I have an appointment."

Sarah tapped her boot harder. "So, how's my mare?" she asked. Her voice was cool, her eyes cooler.

"Your ex-mare is fine. I rode her today without a bridle and saddle." I couldn't resist throwing that in.

"What's the matter? Can't figure out how to tack up

a horse?" She laughed at her own poor joke.

I turned back to the horses in the arena. Mr. Dellins was on a tall, thin Thoroughbred, cantering it in tiny circles. I searched for Nigel but didn't see him.

I could still smell Sarah's perfume. Too sweet, especially for her. "So," I said. "Been busy at night, haven't you?" I looked at her sideways.

"What's that supposed to mean?"

"You touch Khan again, and that'll be the last time."

"Oh, no, Emily. I'm scared now."

"Don't you have anything better to do with your time? She's my mare, so back off."

Sarah threw back her head and laughed, her throat pulsing. I hated her.

"You don't tell me what to do," she said, poking the riding crop into my ribs.

I slapped it away, and the crop flew from her hand.

"Pick it up," she said.

I turned and walked away, bile rising in my throat, my heart racing. I held myself tight and walked slowly and carefully to the other side of the arena and into the barn, hoping to find Nigel.

"Sometimes it's best just to walk away," said a voice from inside a stall. Between iron slats was Nigel and his horse with the white legs. Each stall had a square window, like a porthole, looking into the arena. He must have watched the whole scene.

"Come on in," he said. "Pasha is gentle, even though he's big."

Unbolting the stall door, I walked in. The chestnut whickered at me.

"Your cousin," I said, "let Khan out of her stall."

Nigel looked up from saddling the gelding and said, "I stopped her Friday night. I didn't know she had gone again."

106

I slumped against the wall. "I thought I saw your horse."

"I can try talking to Uncle Bill, but I'm afraid that'll make her madder. She's already upset that you came over today."

"I noticed."

Nigel bridled Pasha, who opened his mouth for the bit. "Perhaps you can lock Khan's door?" he suggested.

"Great. I change my life because Sarah's jealous."

"Look, I'm sorry about it all. Really." He knotted the reins. "Why don't we go look at the stallions now?"

I wanted to trust him, but I didn't know why. Because he was taking time with me and seemed genuinely interested? I wished I could read his mind.

We walked out into the sun, Pasha following like a great dog. Nigel didn't even have hold of him. We walked into the main barn where Mr. Petersen's office was. Sarah seemed to have vanished.

"Two horses are probably best suited for Khan," Nigel said. His voice was like a teacher's, which annoyed me. I wasn't some dumb kid. "Misk is one and El Noor is the other. Misk has pretty good conformation, although he tends to be a little weak in the croup. Personally I prefer El Noor. But they're both well bred."

"Where are you from?" I asked suddenly, pulling a Farley.

"What?"

"Your accent."

He smiled and said, "I didn't think it was noticeable anymore. I've been back for almost three years." He glanced at me, Pasha between us. "I lived in Germany for most of my life."

"Why were your parents in Germany?"

"My dad was German. He rode in Vienna with the Spanish riding school."

My mouth dropped about ninety miles. Then the past tense of his sentence struck me. "Was?"

"Yeah. He was killed about three years ago." He stopped in front of a stall and changed the subject in a false, bright voice. "Here's the first candidate, Misk."

A bright, polished chestnut peered out at us, his forelock a scarlet fringe in his eyes. He snorted, and he and Pasha sniffed at each other. Pasha looked away, bored, but Misk squealed and struck the padded door. "Stop," commanded Nigel. He took down the leather halter with a brass circle engraved with Misk's name, haltered the stallion, and led him out into the aisle. Pasha ambled out of the way and stuck his head over another stall door.

Nigel stretched him, and Misk, rolling his eyes, stood with his back legs extended, his tail flipping over his left hip, a red ripple. "Not bad," he said, walking around the stallion who stood ramrod still, the lead chain hanging in space under his chin. "Clean legs, pasterns not too straight, not cow hocked, nice head and eyes. He throws nice babies."

Taking the chain, Nigel told Misk, "At ease. Relax." The stallion drew his legs back under him and Nigel returned him to the stall. "El Noor is on the other side."

I followed Nigel, feeling like one of his horses. Pasha mosied along after us, still sticking his face into stalls and nickering with the occupants.

"Is he supposed to do that?" I asked.

Nigel gave me another grin. "He's very social. He's not a fighter, and the stallions know that. He's all right."

Nigel opened another stall and led out a stallion. "El Noor," he announced. The stallion walked out as if he were on springs. Most Arabians aren't tall, but he was close to sixteen hands. Pure, shining white, his skin black under the whiteness. *Horses were once stars.* He was the color of starlight, undergirded by the night.

"He's gorgeous," I said.

Nigel stretched him. He was Khan's mate. I knew that immediately. He would sire her foal. "Him," I said. "I want him."

Nigel laughed. "I hope I didn't influence you, but he's my favorite, too. Do you want to ride him?"

"Are you serious?"

"Sure. You're a good enough rider."

"I thought you said I just rode bouncy green horses."

"It's not easy riding colts. On El Noor, you'll think you're in heaven."

I was already in heaven. *I sure hope there are horses in Heaven, God.* In Revelation it talks about Jesus and the armies of Heaven riding on white horses. They were probably related to El Noor.

Nigel held the stallion while I tacked him up English. My fingers trembled a little as El Noor craned his face to gaze at me, his nostril sun red.

"He's a drinker of the wind," I said.

"He's actually imported from Egypt. He looks like your Khan, doesn't he?"

"Yes. Khan will like him."

He laughed. "She'll like any stallion. Mares aren't picky."

"I'll take him," I said. Nigel went to retrieve Pasha down the aisle, still visiting.

We led the horses outside. The winds were still murmuring, louder now, and El Noor twitched his ears all around. "Radar ears," I said.

After we mounted, we rode over to the outdoor course. El Noor moved under me smooth as a sailboat, perfectly on keel.

"He has a light mouth," said Nigel.

I nodded. I put him through his paces. He was

different from the colts. I didn't have to correct him, or explain anything to him, I just softly asked and he trotted, cantered, stopped. Everything. A tremendous sense of energy emanated from him. I thought he could teach me a few things.

I slowed him as Nigel and Pasha took a jump. Pasha leaned into the rails, clearing them neatly, his forelegs tucked to his chest and his tail flagging high in the air.

"Were you jumping him in the dark a few nights ago?" I called as he brought the horse around.

"Was that you? I could tell there was a horse up on the hill, because Pasha was all in a dither. Sometimes a social horse is a pain."

"How can you jump in the dark? You might hurt him."

Nigel shook his head. "Horses have good night sight. It's more than that, though. Pasha and I have, oh, I'm not sure what to call it. Trust, maybe. He can jump blindfolded."

"What does he have, sonar or something?"

"Somehow I can tell him how far to jump. Or maybe he knows. I'm not sure. I've had him since he was a foal. I even watched him being born. I guess we just know each other."

We rode companionably around the jumps, Pasha and Nigel occasionally leaping over a few. "Can you jump?" he asked. "El Noor's not half bad."

"I have, but mostly fooling around. Nothing serious."

"Try." He stopped Pasha next to a low rail.

I circled El Noor and touched him with my heels. He broke into a canter from a fast walk and I aimed him for the center of the rail jump. We strode closer. I raised myself in the stirrups, gave El Noor his head, and the stallion leaped, an arch of light, over the rail. As he hit the tanbark ground, he grunted and bucked.

110

"Wonderful!" called Nigel. "You have a great seat. From riding those idiot babies, no doubt."

I slowed El Noor. "That was fun!"

We walked back to the barn. Nigel detoured and took me around the far side of the ranch, trotting slowly under trees, the light playing through the leaves.

"Did you bring Pasha back from Germany?"

He nodded. "My father helped me train him. I did a good bit of showing there. Dressage. A lot of show jumping."

"You don't now?"

"No." His face started to close up, like it had when I refused to believe him that day at school. I didn't want that to happen, but I didn't know how to stop it.

"My parents are divorced," I said. I knew I was babbling, but I wanted to win his confidence somehow. "But I think that a death would be worse. I mean, at least I can see my mom and write her letters."

"You live with your dad? That's unusual, isn't it?"

"Yeah. We kids didn't want to go with her. She's the one who walked out."

"That's too bad." He patted Pasha. I think he was deciding if he ought to reciprocate stories. Then he said, his accent more pronounced, "My dad was killed because he was in the wrong place at the right time. A bomb went off, and that was it."

"A bomb?"

"We were at a race track in Poland. It was a terrorist bomb. A Soviet official was there, but he wasn't hurt. The thing is, I was standing next to my dad. When the horses came down the home stretch, I ran to the rail and—kapow! If I hadn't moved at that moment, I would have been killed, too."

My hands were cold on the reins. The wind's song had changed to a dirge. "That's terrible, Nigel."

"Yeah, it is. I stopped showing horses because . . . I

111

don't know. It didn't mean anything anymore. Or maybe it meant too much. I'm not sure which."

We were back at the barn, and El Noor pulled at the bit. A stableboy appeared, and as I slid off he took El Noor. I had sort of hoped to put the stallion away myself, maybe talk more with Nigel, but Nigel was half in the barn already. Dismissed, I guess.

Nigel looked back. "Thanks for coming by." He glanced into the barn. "Just for the record, my uncle didn't suggest you come over. It was my idea." He disappeared into the barn with Pasha on his heels.

I walked rapidly home and noticed that the winds had changed their song once more. A warm earth melody. The dirge was gone.

13
Love and Diet Coke

Ian came into my room after I was in bed, a blanket wrapped around him. He lay down on the floor between my bed and the window.

"Are you awake?" he whispered.

I didn't answer. With Ian in my room, I would have more trouble sneaking out to stay in the barn. My sleeping bag was under the bed and the travel alarm clock under my pillow, set for eleven-thirty. I hoped Sarah wouldn't sneak to the barn sooner—I hoped she wouldn't come at all.

Ian turned over and sighed.

The clock ticked under my head. "Ian?"

"I thought you were asleep."

"I'm having a nightmare." Little pun.

"So tell me about it."

I explained about Khan being out, about Sarah, about Nigel, about everything. It was easy to spill it all in the darkness. When I finished, Ian stretched out, his head propped up by his arm.

"Say something," I said finally. "Are you breathing?"

"First, do you have a lock?"

"I think so. From my junior high locker."

"We'll go out and lock her stall. No big deal, Em."

I pulled on jeans over my nightgown. "I hate having to change my life for her."

"So don't." He stopped putting on clothes, his arms half in his shirt. "You risk something else happening to Khan. It's that simple."

I made an impatient noise, but we walked outside to the barn, my old combination lock in my hand. "I hope I remember the numbers." I twirled it and tried a few sets of numbers before it popped open. Khan stuck her face out and breathed down my neck as I locked the latch.

"She is pretty," said Ian. He stroked her fine curved neck.

"I thought you didn't like horses."

"Why do you say that?"

"You never ride or anything."

We headed back to the house, after glancing around and making certain no one was lurking nearby. The stars were crisp.

Ian rubbed his chin. "I spend my time with other things. I like horses all right; I'm just not passionate over them like you are."

Back in my room, I pulled off my stiff jeans and crawled back into bed. The sheets were cold, and I curled up into a ball, my chin almost to my knees. "What are you passionate about?" I asked.

Ian lay down on the floor. "Do you have another blanket? It's freezing down here."

I threw a blanket from the foot of the bed at him, and he spread it out over himself. "I'm passionate about computers."

I laughed. "I knew that already."

"I'm really interested in outer space. I want to be involved in space colonization. Star travel, too, but

114

that's a lot further down the road."

I thought about Nigel and the way his father had been killed. "It seems like a lot is going on here on Earth. Stuff to take care of."

"Wherever you go, there'll be problems. I'm not trying to escape. People like Sarah will be on space colonies, too."

I uncurled a little.

"How about you, Em?"

"I don't know. You and Farley have always known what you'll do. Go off in outer space and do this and that, but me, I don't know. Right now I want to make Sarah stop bothering me, and I want to be friends with Khan."

"I don't know about Khan, but I have a feeling Sarah is going to be a tough cookie."

"She's a creep."

"And you haven't been much better to her."

"Ian!" I sat bolt upright. "I don't do half the things she does."

"So. Even one is bad enough."

"Thanks a lot." I dropped back against my pillow.

"You don't have to be her bosom buddy. Just don't let her get under your skin, Em."

I sighed and thought about Khan in the dewy grass this morning. "I guess so." Ian was quiet. I pulled the clock out from under my pillow and pulled the stem on the alarm, figuring Khan would be fine until morning.

After feeding the horses Monday morning, I walked back to the house. Melissa was sitting at the kitchen table buttering toast and drinking a can of diet Coke while Ian rinsed off his breakfast plates. "So," he was saying, "you're going to be fifteen, eh?"

"Getting up there," she said.

"And you're ready to retire, Ian," I said.

Dad walked into the kitchen. "So where does that place me?"

"Over the hill," said Ian.

"Over the mountain range," I said.

Dad turned to Melissa. "Don't I have nice children? I work my fingers to the bone and get no respect."

I took a can of diet Coke out of the refrigerator and sat down with Melissa, opening my algebra book.

"Really, girls," said Dad. "It's not even eight in the morning, and you're drinking soda?"

"Let them rot their guts," said Ian, stuffing books into his backpack.

"It's no different from drinking coffee," I pointed out.

Dad shook his head and tossed the truck keys to Ian. "When will you be back?"

"My last class is over at two." For our benefit, he added, "Some of us have to go to school."

"You have a tough life, for sure," I said.

Ian smiled angelically and said, "I'll try and make your party, Melissa." He waved and was gone.

"So where's my invitation?" I asked. "Everyone has one but me, the birthday girl's best friend, who doesn't even know what time it starts."

Melissa grinned and slid a square, white envelope across the table. I ripped it open and read quickly. "A masquerade party! Bible characters only! No way. You didn't tell me that."

"It was Brenda's idea. I think it'll be fun."

"That sister of yours has entirely too much influence over you."

Melissa laughed. "But, bummer of the century, Em. Stallion can't come."

"Stallion?" asked Dad, who was leaning against the counter, drinking orange juice and listening to us. "Who on earth is Stallion?"

116

"Oh, this guy at school." I stared at Melissa. "Did you invite him?"

"He must be a real animal," said Dad, and he laughed.

We both ignored him. "I sent him an invitation," said Melissa, "but he called and said he had other plans."

"I can't believe it!" I buried my head in my arms. "You didn't."

"What's the matter?" asked Farley, padding into the kitchen.

Dad turned on the water in the sink. "Oh, your sister's upset because someone named Stallion can't come to Melissa's party."

"Oh, him," said Farley. "He's a dumb guy who plays football."

"Shut up, Farley," I said.

Dad gave me a look.

"How does he even know you?" I asked Melissa.

"He doesn't. I gave an invitation to Jason and mentioned I had a friend who really liked his older brother. . . ."

"You didn't!" My voice shot up.

"Let's go," said Dad to Farley. "This is too much for me."

As they walked through the kitchen door, Farley said, "He's a terrible football player, anyway. He fumbles all the time."

"He does not," I hollered.

"Does too!" The front door slammed shut.

"I didn't mention your name," said Melissa. She tossed back her hair.

"Did you invite the President of the United States, too?"

"Yeah. But his secretary called and said he couldn't come. He has a meeting to attend."

"I see," I said and sipped my Coke. Melissa grinned and shoved her homework across the table. I checked her answers against mine. Not bad; only two wrong. We worked on the ditto sheets, with my calculator.

"Is Ian still going with Laura?"

"I guess. I don't think he's serious about anyone. He wants to finish his degrees first. All his friends are into astrophysics and stuff like that."

"Even Laura?"

"Yeah. Kindergarten physics or something like that. Sub-atomic parts. Quarks. Weird stuff."

Melissa looked down at her paper where she had been sketching a face. When she saw me looking at it, she scribbled it out.

"Why did you do that?" I asked.

"I still want to be an artist. I guess that cancels out marrying your brother."

"Don't be silly. Why would it?"

"Because I couldn't understand the stuff he does. You know I'm terrible in math."

"There's more poetry in physics than you might guess. Besides, if you really love each other, you can make it work." My voice rang in my own head: *What about Mom and Dad? Didn't they love each other enough to make it work?*

"Love conquers all, huh?"

"Don't be sarcastic," I said. "It doesn't become you."

Melissa gave me a crooked smile. "My mom says I borrow trouble. Maybe so. Why did your parents divorce?"

I ran my finger over the beads of moisture on my Coke can. "Maybe it was goals, career."

"Oh, great. Thanks, Em."

"Oh, it was deeper than that. Their outlook was different. My mom wanted different things from my dad, so they split. Then Dad got saved, and that really set Mom off. He tried to get back with her, but no way. She still doesn't like us being 'religious,' as she puts it."

"What happened before that? They just stopped loving each other?"

"I'm not sure." I tried to push my thoughts back in time. My parents never yelled much or argued. It was more of an atmosphere. Like the time I visited in the mountains of New Mexico—I *felt* a storm coming in, silent and furious. "It was like they were walking together at first; then they started up a mountain, only on different sides."

"And your dad tried to get back with her?"

"Yeah, but then Mom was already seeing this other guy." Ian and Farley went to Mom's wedding, but I had refused to go. I don't think she's ever really forgiven me. "My dad prays for my mom. I think that's love."

Melissa ran her fingers through her hair. "Maybe your parents didn't really love each other. Maybe they just thought they were in love."

I said slowly, "Love isn't just a feeling. It's something you decide to do, like—like cleaning a horse stall."

Melissa burst out laughing. "You make it real attractive."

I put my feet up on the opposite chair. "I take care of Khan and the other horses because I love them. And I have to do yucky work with them, too."

"Loving horses and loving people are different."

"Only a matter of degree."

She wrinkled her nose. "This is a heavy conversation. I'll have to take a poll at my house. I can announce the results at my party. Can I quote you?"

She was *The Los Angeles Times* reporter now, flourishing her pen and taking notes.

"Sure, quote me," I said grandly.

"I'll call Stallion and ask his opinion."

"You better not!"

Melissa said, "I invited Nigel Waters, too."

"Why?" I asked, not sure if I was upset or not.

"We needed more guys. I just hope he doesn't bring Sarah."

"You're amazing," I said. "Anyone else I should know about?"

"I just want Ian to be there. That's all I care about."

Whom did I want there? Stallion? Not particularly. I think I liked admiring him from afar. Nigel? Maybe. I was curious about him.

We finished another ditto sheet. Then Melissa went home, and I went out to the barn where a double horse trailer was parked by the trainee barn. Cobol's owner.

Dad and a man I didn't know stood by the sheep pasture, with Cobol haltered and in hand and two new horses in the pasture.

"Emily, this is Cobol's owner, Mr. James," said Dad as I came up, putting my hand on the colt's rump. The colt eyeballed me.

"Hello," I said and held out my hand.

His grip was firm. "So, you're my colt's trainer, eh?" His teeth were very white.

My face grew hot. Dad was smiling. "My dad broke him," I said. "I just put time into riding him."

Mr. James patted Cobol's shoulder. "He's muscled up nice. I like that."

"Tractable," said Dad. "He was good to work with."

"My daughter will probably take him under her wing. She shows, mainly Western Pleasure."

I hoped she was a nice girl.

"Em, why don't you saddle him up and show Mr. James his paces?"

120

"I'd like that." Mr. James showed his white teeth again.

I tacked Cobol up, conscious that this would be the last time, and rode him into the arena where the men waited by the gate. My fingers were cold on the reins, and my stomach was jumpy. I wanted Cobol to look good. I rode him in wide circles, a swinging walk, a strapping trot, a fluid canter. He flowed over the ground, switched leads, not yanking at the bit as he sometimes did.

I looked up to see how the men were reacting, and glimpsed a blur of animal against the fringe of green hills. Cobol stiffened, and his ears shot up. Someone rode deeper into a patch of bushes. I was sure I saw a horse with white legs.

Cobol stumbled and clenched at the bit. "Sorry, boy," I whispered, steadying him.

Dad and Mr. James didn't appear to have noticed.

"Perfect," said Mr. James. "Just perfect."

I halted Cobol before them and backed him a few paces, Cobol tucking his nose and moving willingly. The colt wasn't even sweating. All the riding in the hills paid off.

As we walked back to the barn, I looked over my shoulder. No one was in sight.

"Mr. James is leaving two new horses," Dad said, pointing at the colts in the pasture. A liver bay and a blue roan.

"Nice," I said, reluctant to dismount Cobol. I stroked his neck under his mane, feeling him draw his breaths between my knees, and chew at the bit, playing with the copper rollers. "When your daughter shows him in this area, would you mind telling me? I'd like to watch."

"Of course. I expect to be doing a lot of business with your father. We'll be in contact."

"Thanks." I rode Cobol back to the barn and dismounted, slowly swinging my leg over his rump, both feet hitting the ground. Stripping the tack off, I ran a brush over his dry coat and covered him with a cooler. I leaned against him while he lipped the brush and I murmured stupid, loving endearments to him.

God, is it all right to love a horse? It's easier to love a horse than a person, that's for sure.

Dad and Mr. James talked and filled out papers while I bandaged Cobol's legs for the vanning. The colt kept turning and staring at me with huge eyes.

"You know you're going, don't you?" I whispered. He flared his nostrils and stamped a front foot. I wrapped his tail; he didn't like that and clamped down his tailbone.

"You ready?" asked Dad.

"No," I said.

"He looks ready."

"He is. You asked if I was ready."

"It's hard to let go, isn't it?" Mr. James asked. "I still hate selling my horses, but it's necessary. My daughter and I will treat him gently and well."

I handed him the lead rope, and he led Cobol into the trailer. Cobol suddenly stopped dead, his forefeet on the ramp. I was surprised because we'd practiced loading in and out a million times. The colt's ribs swelled, and he let loose a ringing neigh. Then he scrambled into the van, almost dragging Mr. James behind him. A lump of tears burned in my throat. Mr. James came back out and said, "The colt sends his love." He and Dad shut the tailgate. Then he waved and climbed into the truck and drove off.

Dad put his hand on my shoulder.

"Rats," I said. "I forgot to tell him that Cobol likes having an apple every morning."

We laughed together, and my tears evaporated.

14
Friends and Fights

Each day I rode Khan in the bull pen. On Tuesday I rode her bareback, with a hackamore, in the arena, while Dad watched. Once she acted up, after I had slowed her and talked with Dad. I squeezed my legs to move her, and she leaped as if she were coming out of a starting gate. To my own amazement, I didn't fall.

"We'll work on starting at a normal pace," I said, hanging onto her mane.

"Good idea," said Dad with a smile. Turning Khan around and heading back for the barn, I thought I saw a horse and rider in the hills again, but I couldn't be sure.

The next two days I trained Io, Ariel, and an Appaloosa colt named Flecks. In the fragments of free time, I rode Khan, bareback and in the hackamore. I hoped the hackamore would keep her from remembering the race track and not associate me with that atmosphere. Besides, riding Khan bareback made her sensitive to my shifting weight, and she always tried to come up squarely under me.

Thursday Dad and I went up to the arena. "Let's canter her today," he said. I was afraid a faster gait might remind her she'd been a race horse. She trotted freely while I rode her, not her odd, shuffling trot, and she didn't limp. At a trot she was smooth, flowing, not like some horses who jarred the teeth from my head.

"Canter her," called Dad as we rounded a corner.

"Here goes," I murmured, and she laid back an ear. I moved my weight closer to her withers and loosened the reins. She trotted faster. "Canter, Khan," I said and pressed my legs against her.

She rocked forward, picking up the correct lead as she poured into the turn, molten metal. Her mane flagged in my face. "Easy, easy," I murmured, keeping my legs firm yet loose against her sides. She increased her speed, and I bumped her nose, but the white fence began to blur.

"Steady, steady." The next corner came up, and she slowed a fraction, turning along the fenceline. Instead of straightening her out, I turned her with my knees and the reins, cantering her in small circles, smaller and smaller, until she cantered the speed I wanted. She relaxed, still flowing, her head rising, her ears pricked through the tangle of mane.

I guided her out of the circle, onto a straight line. She rocketed off, not obeying me, not slowing, so I bent her in another circle. She switched leads and cantered in small circles again. Finally I stopped her, sitting back hard. She planted her hooves, dust flinging up under us.

A sheen of sweat lay over her neck, but she wasn't breathing hard. I glanced up at Dad, who stood with someone else holding a horse by the reins. A horse with white legs.

I walked Khan over to them, and she poked her head across the fence. Nigel rubbed her nose.

"How did she feel?" asked Dad.

"Pretty good. She still wants to run, but at least she

let me control her." I picked alfalfa flowers out of her mane.

Nigel rested his hands on the fence. He wore a short-sleeved shirt, and the hair on his arms was blonde. "Would you like to go riding in the hills?" he asked. "Pasha and I are used to spooky horses. Sometimes we pony the babies around with their first riders."

I glanced at Dad, who nodded like it was no big deal. He just said, "Don't go too far, Em. I need you to watch Farley tonight, because Megan and I are going out."

I smoothed down Khan's mane near her withers. "It'll be good for her to get out." I wondered why Nigel was here, but no one except me seemed to think it was extraordinary.

We rode out of the arena. Khan and Pasha swung their heads, gazing at each other unabashedly. I should be so bold.

Instead I said, "Why have you been watching from among the trees? Don't say you haven't, because I've seen Pasha."

The horses trotted down a gentle incline. Nigel said, "I've wondered how Khan was doing."

"Thanks. Don't trust me, huh?"

"Look, I like this mare. I was just wondering."

"I see." I was amused, wondering if he was watching Khan or me.

Khan walked fast, taking long strides. She seemed to like being out. "What do you do at the ranch?" I asked. "I mean, your job?"

"Different things. I coordinate some of the training, especially with the stallions, because of the work I used to do with my dad."

"Did you work with the Lippizzaners?"

"As I got older I did. I wanted to learn the airs above ground, but my dad was killed." He shrugged, his face

125

lifted to the breeze. I could imagine him riding the high school level of dressage, the kind of riding that so few people or horses attain. "I don't know if I'll get the chance again."

I didn't know what to say—sorry wasn't enough. Pasha picked his way over rough ground, and Khan followed briskly. When Mom and Dad got divorced, people stammered around, trying to give comfort. Instead they embarrassed us. Or they'd give us kids long, pitiful looks. That was worse. You'd think we'd been turned into toads, and no one knew the right spell to change us back. I suspected that Nigel, too, had had his share of lame words and mournful looks.

"My mom and I came back to the States after Dad was killed. My mom is Uncle Bill's sister. We stayed with them a while. I'm not sure why, but Uncle Bill has let me work his horses. I think that's what has saved my sanity."

Nigel guided Pasha off the worn trail and onto a rumpled, green hillside. I followed without questioning, curious. Khan picked up her hooves carefully, her head low, swerving around tree roots and rocks. Nigel glanced back once, so I urged Khan up beside Pasha.

"Do you ever show Mr. Petersen's horses?" I asked.

He shook his head. "No, and he's mad at me for not showing. In fact, he's got a bunch of horses back east now. Hunters, jumpers, a few eventers. Uncle Bill and I go through this every year. But I don't want to show."

I wanted to say something, something to wipe away his unease, his sorrow. "Did you know that stars sing?" I asked him.

He gave me a funny look, a smile beginning in his eyes. "Do they?"

"I've never heard them, but radio astronomers say different stars emit different sounds."

126

"I'd like to hear stars sing," he said. "They must sound beautiful."

Acceptance. I felt like he'd taken a tiny gift from me.

We rode down into a fold of hills where a thin stream tumbled out from behind a pile of granite, black and white jumbled together. The water curled through the narrow valley and vanished into the ground, seeping through the loose soil.

"I don't know much about stars," Nigel said, slowing Pasha, "But I do know flowers, and I've found some very different ones. I thought you might like them." He said it offhandedly, but I felt that the flowers—his gift—were important.

Nigel leaned over Pasha's crest. "See? Under those oaks?"

I pushed Khan closer and hung over her side. She turned her face and nibbled at my boot. Small white and red flowers freckled the ground, pushing up through the thick layers of brown soil, sticking their small faces near the trees' gnarled roots. The flower petals were half-moon shaped, seven to each stalk. A faint scent tickled my nose.

I sat back up and shook my hair from my eyes. "I've never noticed them before. Or this place."

"That's what I like about these hills. I always find new things in them," he said.

A verse I had memorized last year in Megan's class surfaced. *I lift my eyes to the hills. From where does my strength come? From the Lord. . . .* Although it isn't about horses, I like it.

"I haven't been able to identify the flowers. I've been meaning to send a sample to Cal Poly and see if they can."

I peered closer. "Farley would probably say that a unicorn had been here."

Nigel laughed softly. "In Germany, I knew some villagers who believed in magical creatures."

I hesitated, then said, "I don't believe in magic, but I believe there are forces at work in the world . . . for good and for evil. But the good is stronger, and it's going to win."

"I think it is, too," Nigel said, his accent strong. We looked at each other for a moment. His eyes were blue, so blue, circles of water, very deep. I wondered what he was thinking, staring back at me, and I didn't want to stop gazing at him. I looked away, hating myself for turning, but if I hadn't I would have pushed Khan closer and put my arms around Nigel's neck. And I didn't want that—yet.

Nigel gave a small sigh. I looked over at him.

"Sarah," he said.

I sputtered mentally, searching for something to say.

Nigel twined his fingers in Pasha's mane. "Sarah thinks she owns me," he said. "It's going to hurt her, finding out that she doesn't."

I clenched the rope reins. "Why does she think she owns you?"

"Once I was content, more or less, to be surrounded by her. I was crushed by my dad's death. After Mom and I came back from Germany, Sarah comforted me. But she has to learn I'm not hers. No one has that right." He looked into my eyes.

I looked back, wishing that Sarah didn't have to intrude every time I was with Nigel. This time Nigel looked away.

We rode out of the valley, the horses straining to make the sharp grade. The light was laying down broad strips of red and gold over the hillsides. As we drew closer to home, we chatted quietly.

"Are you going to Melissa's party?" he asked.

"Of course. She's my best friend."

"What are you going to dress up as?"

"I'm not sure. Maybe one of those four living creatures. They have all these eyes and six wings."

He had a blank look on his face. "Huh?"

"Don't you know the Book of Revelation?"

"I guess not."

"It's the last book in the Bible. It has these great creatures who sit around God saying, 'Holy, holy, holy.' Melissa draws them sometimes. They're great looking."

"Sounds like science fiction."

"Better."

At our place, I turned Khan for the barn. Night was nearly here, and Megan and Dad would be going out soon.

"Thanks for showing me the flowers," I said. Khan pushed out her nose, wanting to go to her stall and eat. I gently pulled her back, and she stamped.

"See you around," Nigel said. Pasha moved into the night, his hooves clicking. Then they were gone.

Khan stamped again.

"You behave," I said. "If I want to wait here a minute, I will."

She shook her head sideways, her mane flying back and forth. She pushed her nose out, but I brought her head back into the proper position.

"Now, Khan," I began, when she reared up, her mane dashing into my face. I let loose of the reins and clutched at her mane. She reared higher, her body swaying back. I threw my weight forward, trying to unbalance her so she'd land on all fours. The longer she stayed up, the more my legs slid over her damp coat. Finally she came down on all fours, snorting. She whirled, and I popped off over her shoulder and landed on my rear end.

Khan thundered off for the barn, reins flying. I scrambled up, dusting off my pants, and headed after her. She stood blowing outside her stall, the other horses rushing up to touch noses with her—wanting to hear the latest gossip, no doubt.

"You're in trouble," I said and walked past her into the tack room. I wasn't going to let her get the best of me. She let out a rolling snort as I reappeared with a bareback pad. It would give me traction to stay on when she reared again.

She let me grab the reins and cinch up the bareback pad, bright red on her gray coat. She snorted again as I led her away from the barn and remounted, swinging my leg over her tense rump, settling smoothly against her. One thing I didn't want to do was fight her, rile her up. I patted her neck and talked to her for a minute; then I squeezed my legs, and she walked back to the place where she had reared. I halted her.

Nigel was probably home now. I was glad he hadn't seen Khan unload me. Khan gazed at the barn, and I looked over at our house. Dad's bedroom light flicked on. He was probably getting dressed to take Megan out to dinner. I wondered what they talked about—things like Nigel and I talked about? Stars, horses, people? I couldn't imagine my dad doing anything other than ordering us kids around or training horses.

Khan stamped her hoof, and I tightened my grip on her mane. *Dear Lord, please don't let her go over backwards, or if she does let me get out of her way.*

"You behave," I said. "You'll get your dinner in a minute."

She shook her head, her mane flying, backlit by the faint sunlight. At least she gave fair notice before she exploded. Some horses simply erupted. Khan laid back her ears and watched me out of her left eye.

"You're not so different from anyone else," I told

her. "You just want your own way."

She crabstepped, then reared, her back muscles tightening.

I leaned forward. My fear rose up with her as her head snaked in the air. Her front hoofs flashed, silently rushing; then she came back down with a hump in her back, and up flew her hind legs. I clapped my legs tighter, bumping with the hard jar. She whirled, and I slipped sideways. Suddenly she came up under me, like a wave under driftwood, and held still, panting.

"Round one," I said and walked her in a figure eight, waiting for her to rear again or buck. She didn't, so I cooled her off and put her inside her stall.

I rubbed her down while she munched her hay. "Still friends?" I asked. She sniffed at my fingers, then buried her face back in the hay.

I guess she was testing me. Lots of the colts did that—tried to get away with things, biting or kicking, maybe running away with the rider. When Khan was a race horse, she must have gotten away with little things, misbehaving until she flipped coming out of the starting gate.

I patted her shoulder and left to the sound of her teeth snapping hay stalks.

15
Bright Day of Rain

Dad had gone out to dinner when I returned to the house. Ian was in his room, muttering and messing with his computer, so I sat in the kitchen with Farley, who was eating popcorn. His flu was gone. Privately, I thought it was mentally induced.

I pulled off my riding boots and put my feet up on the chair. "Khan and I had our first real fight."

"Kevin and I fight," Farley said. "All friends fight. But Kevin and I make up." He stuffed more popcorn into his mouth.

I told him about riding in the hills with Nigel, though I didn't say anything about wanting to hug him. Just thinking about it made me hot and embarrassed.

"Anyone who likes stars is okay," he said.

"I doubt it's that simple."

Farley licked the butter off his fingers. "Nigel likes stars and horses, so I'd say he has two points on his side."

I swirled some unpopped kernels around in the bottom of the bowl, wondering why people, and horses, were so complicated.

"I'm going to spend the night at Kevin's on Saturday. Dad says it's okay because you're going to Melissa's party and Ian's going up to Mt. Wilson. I don't want to be here when Dad and Megan have dinner."

"Don't you like Megan? Have you asked her if she likes stars?"

He gave me a dirty look. "I don't care if she likes stars. I don't want to be here Saturday night."

I didn't push it. "You'll have fun at Kevin's. And then we'll all see each other at church."

Sunday would be Easter. It didn't used to be my favorite holiday, because I didn't get any presents, but since I became a Christian I began to see that Easter was like a rainbow, shimmering, layers of colors.

"Yeah," Farley said. He ate more popcorn. "I like Easter because it's not hidden behind bows and junk. It's a bright day even if it rains."

Ian straggled into the kitchen. "Hey, you ate all the popcorn!"

"Sorry, Your Majesty," I teased and got up to pop more. Although it was night, I could feel and see that it was actually a bright day.

Friday I test-rode Khan to Melissa's and let the mare prowl the old corral next to the backyard. Khan spent a long time sniffing the wooden rails.

"She must smell Seth's steer," said Melissa.

We stood in the backyard watching her trot restlessly, then stop and take a long drink from the trough.

"Who are you going to be for my party?" asked Melissa.

"Wrong question," I said. "Not *who*, but *what* will I be?"

"Emily! Please come halfway normal." She took a swing at me, and I jumped back. Khan started.

"You're scaring my horse," I teased.

"And you're scaring me. Just don't come dressed like one of those four living creatures."

She knew how much I loved those guys. Actually, I couldn't figure out how to attach all those wings. The eyes I could draw and pin onto a sheet, but the wings threw me. "Well," I deliberated, "if you insist. Maybe I'll come as a rider in the army of God. They ride on white horses, you know." I pointed to Khan, who was more dappled silver than white.

"Couldn't you be a human?"

"Too common."

"Come on, Emily. You're my best friend. I don't want to walk around all night with a six-winged, many-eyeballed creature."

I laughed and sat down on the little fence that separated the lawn from the slope that rose up to a five-foot stake fence.

"Okay," I said. "I'll try and think of a human. How about King David? I could buy a fake beard—"

"A *female* human, please?"

Melissa sat down next to me, and we laughed until Khan gazed curiously at us, her ears upright, eyes bright.

"Okay, okay," I promised. "I'll be a female human."

Khan prowled around the corral longer and then settled down to graze. I rode her home and she behaved herself, even when a car roared past.

That night we went to the Good Friday service. Megan didn't sit with us because she was in the choir. I sat between Dad and Ian. Melissa and her family sat in the pew in front of us. It felt good to be there. I felt like I belonged—in church, with my family, with God.

Melissa smiled over her shoulder as the service

finished. "See you tomorrow," she said.

Saturday was busy. We all worked at the barn, stripping the stalls completely and laying down fresh bedding. Bottom watched me unblinkingly, nodding as if to say, *Good job, child*.

"Do you think I'm your servant, you goat?"

He lifted his upper lip, a horse laugh.

When we finished at the barn, I put Khan out in the sheep pasture to take the edge off her, so she wouldn't be crazed at Melissa's party. She bucked and pranced under the sunlight, corking her body like a rodeo horse.

"Bucking bronc," I said. Dad leaned on the fence, watching with me. Khan grunted and squealed, rearing beside Bottom, who looked surprised. He gave a few half-hearted bucks, his knee popping.

"You be careful with her tonight," said Dad.

"I'm not riding far."

"A lot can take place in a little space."

"I'll be okay."

Khan came up to the fence. "You'll be a good girl, won't you?" I asked. She wheeled and trotted back to Bottom, who drowsed in the sunlight. I watched the fog fan in from the mountains, long and lazy like streams, the color of Khan, then I went to ride Ariel and Io.

Late that afternoon, Farley sat on my bed with his small, canvas suitcase, watching me get ready for the party. "Who are you?" he asked.

I draped a blue sheet over my shoulder, studying myself in the mirror. I'd smudged eyeliner around my eyes, trying to look dark and mysterious. I looked about as mysterious as Mother Goose.

"I'm Abigail. I'll ride Khan, though in the Old Testament, Abigail rode on a donkey."

135

"Who was Abigail, anyway?"

"She had this stupid husband who made King David mad. She stopped David from killing her husband and everyone else."

"Are you going to dress up Khan?"

I nodded and pinned the sheet so it lay over one shoulder and came up around my head. Abigail probably wore a hood because of the desert winds.

The doorbell rang, and I heard Ian answer, greeting his friends from Cal Tech. He had already picked up Laura. Poor Melissa.

Farley scrutinized me, holding He-Man around the head. "Wouldn't it be funny if He-Man went back in time to see King David? He-Man could be a Christian then."

I buckled two glittery belts around my waist and tried not to laugh. "There weren't any Christians then. Jesus hadn't come."

"What were they?"

"Israelites."

"Oh. Well, He-Man could go back to Jesus' time and be a Christian."

"Why are you so concerned about He-Man?" I asked, brushing my hair. I had braided it wet and let it dry, so now it was crinkly.

He set He-Man on Battle Cat. "I just am. Kevin and I play that He-Man gets saved."

"I didn't know Kevin believed in God."

"I don't think he does. But he likes He-Man to get saved. Sometimes we blow He-Man up, and he goes to Heaven. It's fun."

"Farley!" Dad hollered. "Let's go."

Farley jumped off the bed, grabbing He-Man and his suitcase.

"See you tomorrow," I called.

Farley stopped in my doorway and started out my

door. He said seriously, "You look beautiful, Abigail. I'm sure King David will think so."

"Thank you, kind sir." Who was my King David? Whose mind did I need to change with kindness? Not Nigel's. Sarah's, then? Maybe.

In the living room, the radio changed to a rock station, so I knew Dad had gone. I stared at myself in the mirror, braiding a strand of clear red beads into my hair. I had a bag of fake gems and silky tassels for Khan, to make her look more the part of a Middle Eastern horse. I walked into the living room, my sheet dragging on one side.

"You look ravishing," said Ian's friend Nicholas, pushing up his glasses and giving me a hug. He stepped back, his hands on my arms. "Let me guess. Esther?"

Ian must have told them Melissa's party was biblical costume. I shook my head no.

Nicholas' girlfriend, Kate, was dark, tall, and slender. "Bathsheba?" she guessed, tossing back her long hair.

"Close. Abigail."

"Oh, ho," said Nicholas. "The peacemaker. That's a good role for you."

It was kind of him to say so. I didn't feel peaceful. I pointed to the back of the sheet. "I can't get this part to stay up."

Kate fixed the sheet, and I smiled over her shoulder at Laura. She had dark red hair and huge blue eyes in a face with a creamy complexion. I thought Melissa was prettier.

"How's your new horse?" asked Laura.

"Okay. I'm going to ride her to the party." I held up the bag of gems and tassels. "I'm going to fix her up and then go."

"We'll see you there," said Ian. "I want to stop by." He turned to Laura. "Melissa's a good kid."

137

Melissa would die with shame if she heard Ian say that, but I guess he had to justify what he was doing for Laura's sake.

The sun was almost down. Grayish-purple streaks slid across the sky, giving it a bruised look. The fog was thicker, but stars peered through the rents. I walked to the barn, wondering how Abigail must have felt walking across the sand to get her donkey to ride out and meet those angry men.

Khan hung her head over the Dutch door. I whirled the lock and opened the door. She sniffed at my sheet and at the bag of jiggly jewels, lipping at them through the bag.

"You'll be a real Arabian tonight," I said.

I wrapped her hackamore with silky cords and tied a string of red gems so they hung along the noseband. I brushed her and recombed her mane and tail, braiding gems into them. Khan shook her head, and the rubies and sapphires tinkled. Instead of reins, I attached a thick red cord.

I led her out and she stepped proudly, her head high, her neck arched. Instead of carrying bread and food like Abigail did, I carried Melissa's birthday present: an art book, oversized, with glossy pictures. Ian helped me pick it out at his campus bookstore weeks ago. She'd love it.

I mounted from the fence, careful not to mess up my outfit. I touched Khan with my legs and she moved forward, jumping when the wind caught the sheet and billowed it. But she wasn't really scared, just looking for an excuse to play.

Her hooves made a satisfying clink-clank on the pavement. Dad had finally shod her front feet, but left her back ones bare, because she had tough hooves. She seemed to enjoy the noise and set down her front feet hard. *Silly horse*, I thought.

A car whizzed by. I wondered if the driver was thinking, *Silly girl*. I must have looked a bit unusual.

Melissa's house was ablaze with lights. I rode Khan up the front drive, past the plum tree, and halted her to get off and open the back gate. Before I could dismount, a familiar voice cut through the night.

"Look who's here."

Khan and I both turned. Sarah stood next to her father's fancy truck, and Nigel was with her.

16
Through the Corral Gate

I clenched my teeth until the wires in my retainer cut my gums. I didn't want to start a fight, not on Melissa's birthday. Besides, I'd only be giving Sarah what she wanted.

Nigel stood near the front door in a puddle of shadows. "Sarah," he said softly. "Let's go."

"I want to see Khan," she said and walked closer. Mr. Petersen drove off, but not before catching my gaze and giving me a terse wave. I knew he was telling me to remember my promise: be nice to his daughter.

Sarah came closer and Khan shook her head, jingling underneath me.

"She's nervous tonight," I said. "It might be better if you don't touch her."

Sarah lifted her face, her fine, spun-gold curls touching her shoulders. Her elegant greenish-gold jumpsuit made me feel like a scullery maid in my sheet and fake gems. I hated her for it.

"Who are you supposed to be?" asked Sarah. "Lawrence of Arabia?"

I had to get out of there before I exploded. Dismounting, the artbook clutched awkwardly under my arm, I opened the back gate and led Khan through. Sarah reached out and touched Khan's mane. The mare recoiled and sprang through the gate, dragging me after her.

"You leave my mare alone," I said, pulling Khan to me. She came, blowing and watching Sarah.

"Don't worry," said Sarah. She laughed. "I don't want your horse."

Shutting the wooden gate, I remounted Khan, wrapping my legs against her warm shoulders, and rode her into the floodlights flaring across the grass.

"Emily," cried Melissa. She slid back the glass door and ran out, looking as pretty as the Queen of Sheba, crown and all. Probably Brenda's old debutante stuff.

Khan shuffled at Melissa's shoulder. "Khan looks great," said Melissa. "So do you. I'm so glad you didn't come as the four living creatures."

Kids gathered at the door, looking out, talking and gesturing. Khan stared warily at them.

I leaned down. "Sarah's here. Did you know that?"

"Are you kidding?" Her smile faded.

"I can't believe it. Nigel was with her."

"Maybe she bugged him into bringing her?" That was Melissa, always giving people the benefit of the doubt.

"It doesn't matter," I said. I wanted Melissa to have a good time. "Shall I show off Khan?"

Melissa ran back to open the glass door and let the kids spill out, oohing and ahing.

I wheeled Khan and she pivoted, her tail flying. We trotted over the lawn and then spun around again. My hood fell back and my hair flung free as Khan broke into a collected canter. The jewels in her mane looked real in the bright lights. Khan was a drinker of the wind and I was her lowly rider, thankful she allowed me to be a part of her.

"Beautiful," someone called.

"Where did you get her?" said another.

Everyone was quieter now. I slid off Khan and led her to the adjoining corral. I pulled off the hackamore, and Khan dropped her head to graze. In the quiet darkness, away from the floodlights, the glitter of the gems vanished and her splendor fell away.

The kids drifted back inside, but I stood a moment, still seeing the desert stretching out, feeling the hot blast of the winds. Khan grazed methodically, the gems clicking together when she moved her face. I left her to eat and went into the house.

Music thrummed, loud and new wave. Blue, green, and red streamers were interwoven overhead, and balloons hung on the ends of the crepe paper. Bowls of dip and chips, platters of fruit and cheese lay on the coffee table. And a huge chocolate cake and brimming punch bowl were on a table near the stairs.

Suddenly I was ravenous. Bruce, a boy from my English class, walked over. He was a clown, always saying outrageous things and breaking up the class.

"Don't tell me, I'll guess," he said. He poured punch into two cups and handed me one. "You're Sheena, Queen of the Jungle." He wore a leopard tunic and sandals, and looked like Farley's He-Man.

"Wrong," I said. "Try Abigail, King David's wife. She was probably a little before Sheena's time."

He laughed and scooped up a handful of chips. "I'm Conan. That was about as biblical as I could get."

A burst of laughter rolled across the basement. Bruce and I turned. In the center of the room, running on all fours, was Nigel, wearing a long, matted wig and a shredded tunic. His arms and legs were bare and sooty. He scrambled around, growling. Even Sarah, sitting between two guys, was laughing.

"Baalam's mule!" someone shouted.

Nigel sat up on his haunches and scratched his arm-pit like an ape. He had smeared something dark over his face.

The guesses flew in.

"Tarzan!"

"Master of the Universe!"

"My sister!"

Everyone laughed. Bruce said, "I think he's from another planet. Planet of the Apes."

Nigel continued scampering around on his hands and knees.

Hmmm. I called out, "Nebuchadnezzar, when he was like an animal covered with dew."

Nigel jumped to his feet. "Emily wins."

"How did you know that?" someone asked. "They must have been in on it together."

"Does she get a prize?" asked Bruce. "That's what's important."

Nigel grinned at me. "A prize, huh?" He came closer, putting his hands on my shoulders. I could tell he was going to kiss me, and I twisted away. He was laughing. "Don't you want your prize?"

"No, I don't want a prize."

"Later," he said and turned away. My face burned.

"Who was that guy?" demanded Bruce. "All these years I've been madly in love with you. . . ."

"Shut up, Bruce," I said and marched away. In sixth grade we sat next to each other, and he used to bring me pretty stones and shells. He was crazy. Bruce gave a mournful howl as kids moved aside to let me through to Melissa.

A pile of colorful presents was stacked on a table. "Lots of loot," I said.

"Did you and Nigel have that planned?" she asked.

"No way." My face flushed again, thinking about him trying to kiss me. I pointed at the present I'd brought. "Ian helped pick it out."

I moved around, talking with lots of people, the costume sheet swirling about my legs like a long, fancy dress. I steered clear of Sarah and Nigel, though a few times I turned and caught him looking at me.

Food kept appearing, so naturally I had to eat it. We cut the cake, and Melissa ripped open her presents. She clutched the artbook from Ian and me to her chest. "Thanks," she said, her eyes shining. "I'll look at it later."

After that, I checked on Khan. She was still grazing peacefully. A few of the jewels had slid through her mane and lay gleaming on the grass. As I picked them up and rebraided them in her mane, some kids came outside and leaned against the fence, watching.

"She's a pretty horse," said a girl from my history class.

"Thanks."

"Feels great out here," said a guy coming through the open door. Khan watched him intently. Others followed, murmuring in agreement. They had on what looked like chain mail. They were probably roasting.

I went back in, struggled with the sliding door a minute. It was always coming off the track. Finally I shut it.

Melissa grabbed my arm. "Ian's here," she said.

My brother walked down the stairs. At the top, Nicholas caught my eye and waved. He and Kate and Laura stood above, waiting for Ian.

I sat down on the floor with a diet Coke, and Melissa went to greet Ian.

"That your brother?" asked a voice in my ear. Nigel sat down beside me.

"Yeah," I said. "Melissa's had a crush on him since I can't remember when."

"Looks mutual," he said.

Ian held out his arms and gave Melissa a big hug. I grabbed some chips. "I suppose if Melissa married him, it wouldn't be too horrible. She'd be my sister-in-law."

Nigel looked amused. "Is it so horrible, getting married?"

I made a face. "I can't imagine anyone wanting my brother." I noticed Sarah watching us from the couch. Little spy. "Why is Sarah here?" I asked.

The humor left Nigel's face. "She was invited."

"Not by Melissa. And it's her party." I hated the way I sounded. Snobbish and self-righteous.

"I invited her."

You had no right, I thought, but I held back the words. "If you'll excuse me," I said, "I need to see my brother."

Nigel's eyes drilled into my back, but I forced myself to walk calmly.

Ian slapped my shoulder, his other arm still around Melissa. "Hi, Em," he said. I punched him, relieved to do something normal. "Looks like a great party," he continued, "but we're on our way to Mt. Wilson to use the telescopes." He let go of Melissa and trooped away with his friends.

Melissa's eyes glowed. "He made the whole party."

"You're hopeless," I said. "Utterly hopeless."

"Who was that?" a girl asked, as we walked back into the cluster of kids.

Bruce called, "Was that my competition, Melissa?"

"He doesn't quit," I said, and we giggled.

About nine-thirty a new batch of kids showed up, coming from a movie, and the basement packed out. I glanced out the glass door to check on Khan. Some kids were on the fence. She half reared, and kids scattered.

"What's going on?" I muttered, pushing my way

145

through knots of people. Between kids, I saw Khan rear again. A figure in greenish-gold stood near her. The mare backed up quickly, her ears back.

I pushed hard for the door, and Nigel instantly appeared. "What's wrong?" he asked.

"Sarah's frightening Khan."

Khan leaped through the open corral gate—who had opened it?—and dashed into the backyard. Hooves clattered over the sidewalk, above the music. Khan thundered up, Sarah behind her, raising a long stick. The dreaded whip.

I yanked at the glass door, but it jammed again on its tracks.

From behind Nigel yelled, "Watch out!"

He hauled me back, as he'd done the day he pulled me away from Stallion. I fought to break away, the sheet tangling my legs. Nigel tripped, and we sprawled together.

Khan came closer to the door, her eyes rolling. I pulled myself away from Nigel as Khan reared again, her hooves scraping the glass door.

Kids screamed. Nigel grabbed me, protecting me as Khan reared higher.

17
Night Hunt

I screamed, "Whoa, Khan, whoa!" but my breath was squeezed out by Nigel's weight.

Khan began lowering her body as if to drop to all fours. A flash of greenish-gold caught my eye. Khan saw it, too. She leaped, as if jumping to safety. She crashed through the glass doors, her forefeet coming in first, like a foal's hooves breaking the birth sac.

Glass shattered in loud, explosive cracks. Kids screamed and ran. Khan charged in, her head, shoulders, sides, flanks, crashing through the shattered door.

I squirmed free of Nigel and scrambled to my feet. Glass rocketed when Khan hit the wooden floor. She slid on her haunches, scattering shards of glass. One struck my cheek. I wiped at my face, and blood stained my fingers.

Kids ran up the stairs, still screaming. Khan slid farther into the basement and threw her head up, trying to regain her footing. Her hind quarters boomed down. She squealed angrily, gathered herself, and stood, shaking.

"Khan," I said and started for her. The basement

was quiet. Someone had killed the music. Khan was bleeding in a half a dozen places. Thin lines of red. A jagged slash on her shoulder. "Easy, girl. Easy."

As if she suddenly realized she was in an unfamiliar place, she snorted and dodged, striking a coffee table with her hind leg. It tipped over with a crash, the food smashing to the floor. She whirled, hitting me, knocking me down onto the glass. She gave a leap and vanished back through the broken doors.

I picked myself up and ran after her. "Wait, Khan. Whoa!" I ran past Sarah, who stood alone with her fist against her mouth. Her eyes were horrified. "I'll kill you for this," I screamed.

Khan galloped across the grass, her hooves slashing the dirt, sinking deep in the grass. She heaved herself up the terrace, increasing her speed. Blood flew back, spattering my face.

I knew what she was going to try. "Whoa, Khan!"

The fence. Solid. Five-feet high. Pointed stake tops. If I could reach her, swing on her back, I could control her.

I tore off the sheet, running as fast as I could. Then Khan froze—an image caught in a camera—and, as if she sucked up all her strength, she sprang from a standing position.

I clenched my hands as she cleared the fence top with her forelegs. But her back legs caught on the top, and her hooves and hocks hit the boards with a deep thump. She cleared the fence, her head ducking from the impact, as she spilled over. *Oh, Khan.* Her hooves hit the packed dirt on the other side of the fence. She grunted when her body hit the ground. Between slats, I saw her rise, stand a moment, and then bolt.

I raced past Melissa for the gate.

"Hurry, Emily!" she called. Oh, and it's her birthday. *I'm so sorry, Melissa.*

I flung open the gate. Some kids had climbed on the fence. Bruce, perched on top, shouted, "She's heading for your place."

Khan's tracks, deep, led toward home. Little spatters of dark liquid pooled in the dirt. I ran and ran, following the tracks up the hill to our house. As I crested our hill, Khan was cresting the hill beyond, the link between the city and the hills. I gasped for breath. She must have jumped the pasture gate.

Oh, God. Burning tears filled my eyes, and angrily I wiped them away. I had to get a horse and go after her. How badly was she bleeding?

No one was home. If only Dad were here, or Ian. Even Farley. I quickly changed into my jacket and jeans and ran out of the house. There wasn't time to write a note to Dad. Melissa would tell him if I didn't get home first.

At the barn, I woke Io. Quickly I tacked him up and tied an extra halter and rope to the saddle. Suddenly we heard footsteps.

"Who's there?" I demanded.

"Me." Nigel's voice. "I've tracked loose horses before."

I almost sent him away, but I knew he wasn't responsible for Sarah. "Okay," I said and led Ariel out for him. Together we tacked the filly up and silently mounted, heading out the sheep pasture for the hills.

"Khan's terrified," I said, after opening the pasture gate. "How else could she have jumped this fence, too?"

"Terrified horses run a long time."

"Don't say that."

The night was foggy. The moon was hiding, leaving only the stars, drops of thin light in the vast darkness. Io slowed at the hilltop, Ariel beside him. Khan could have fled in any direction.

Nigel dismounted, holding the reins, and knelt. "I wish I had brought a flashlight. But I think she continued along this trail."

He climbed back on. Io strode through the thick air.

"Usually injured animals go off by themselves," Nigel said.

Injured animals. Great. *Please don't let her bleed to death.* I burst out, "Why did you invite Sarah?"

He sighed impatiently. The saddle creaked. "Because she wanted to come. Her feelings were hurt that she didn't get an invitation, but everyone else did."

Melissa probably would have invited her, except for me. Io bobbed his head. "Why would Sarah do that? She had a stick. Khan thought it was a whip. . . ." I bit my lower lip so I wouldn't cry.

"I know. She wants attention."

"I guess it worked."

"Look, Emily. I told you she has a rotten home life."

"Everyone's got problems," I muttered. Even to myself I sounded cold.

Nigel said, "So you're able to deal with your frustrations less aggressively. Some people can't. I'm not saying Sarah was right. It's just the way she responds. You ought to know, the way you two have been at each other's throats all these years."

His words irritated me. The wind had picked up, whirling in from the north. My face and fingers were numb. Was Khan cold?

Inside my jacket I was warm, yet deeper inside the cold penetrated. All I could think of was Khan. *Please, God, let me find her. Soon.* Melissa's prayer, in front of her house before I owned Khan, seemed like a hundred years ago. "Let Emily care for Khan like in Proverbs." I knew Melissa would be praying for me now, and that made me feel better.

"Where do you think she might go?" Nigel asked.

"Some place she thought was safe."

"Were would that be?"

"I don't know. If I knew, I'd hide there occasionally, too."

We rode silently, except to make suggestions. "Ride between those bushes," or "Let's take this path." The wind increased, tugged the fog around, ocean foam in the sky. The horses crossed a valley thick in fog. Khan could be here, and we'd never know it. I called her name, and occasionally Io neighed. He and Ariel listened, but an answer never came.

Tiredness washed against me. The plunge after an adrenalin high. I closed my eyes, but instead of peaceful nothingness, I saw Khan, pearly gray in sunlight. Where was she? Would she run blindly or actually head some place in particular? For home? Where was her home? Not our place, yet. Certainly not the Petersens'. Some horses have a strong instinct to return to their home range. That would be Florida. Would she head east?

"Does that help?"

I jerked my head up, opening my eyes. "What?"

"Praying. Wasn't that what you were doing?"

"Sort of, I guess. God knows where Khan is."

Nigel said, "But He won't tell?"

"God?" I hurried Io next to Ariel. "God isn't some genie to get spells and stuff from. He does things His own way." I couldn't resist giving him a curious glance and asking, "What do you think about God?"

He let out his breath slowly. Ariel cocked back an ear, and he patted her shoulder. "Most of the time I believe Someone, Something created all this. I mean, there are so many kinds of flowers. I think Someone must have put time and care into creating it all. But I'm still trying to figure out if there's Someone who cares about us and stuff that happens to us."

"Like finding Khan."

"Yeah. And about my cousin. And my dad. Why he was killed. Why I wasn't. I've thought maybe I wasn't killed for a reason. Maybe that's too self-centered. I don't know."

We dropped down a hillside. "How about you?" he asked lightly, but I felt the tension beneath.

"Do you know anything about stellar evolution?" I asked.

Nigel looked surprised. "A little. Our sun will die. Turn into a red giant. Then a white dwarf."

"That's the way a star should be. I mean, it's lived for something. It's shone on planets and helped life. Ian taught me about them for a science project in seventh grade, just after Mom split. He explained about red giants sitting on horizontal branches, white dwarves, neutron stars. Some stars," I continued, my voice cutting across the darkness, "don't live like that. They don't fulfill anything. They don't have enough mass, and they start collapsing before they become stars. They die as brown dwarves. I . . . I didn't want to be like that."

He said, "You were afraid you'd be nothing."

"Worse than that. Like I could have had all these chances, but failed, because I wasn't willing to become a star. I don't know, Nigel. Maybe it sounds corny, but it was how I felt. Left behind. And scared of what I wasn't. That's what pushed me toward God."

"Now you're a star, shining."

I laughed and put my face in Io's mane, cold and shivery. "I suppose so. Farley says we're all made of 'star stuff.' "

We climbed off the horses to stare at the ground. Tracks were everywhere, mostly old. A few fresher

152

looking ones seemed to take the fork to the left. The starlight was dim. I rubbed my eyes and swung back up. We rode along the path.

"The first time I saw you, when you were rescuing Khan, I was so mad that you were Sarah's enemy. She had always talked about this girl named Emily. I wasn't sure who you were. Then I saw you, and I liked you, but I hated you for being her enemy."

"I didn't want to be her enemy. She forced me into it."

Nigel didn't answer.

"All right," I admitted. "It's my fault, too."

"Don't you wonder why she's the way she is?"

I tightened my lips. "Honestly, Nigel. I don't have time. I can hardly keep up with her, trying to guess what she'll do next." The image of Khan crashing through the glass crashed into my mind, and I put my heels to Io. We had to find Khan. Ariel's hooves clicked after us.

The sky, if possible, was darker.

"Darkest before dawn," said Nigel, reading my mind. "It's darker in Germany. Especially in the forests."

"Why?"

"Not as many city lights. More country."

The horses strode toward the taller hills. I never rode here. It was far from home. The night was different here. Fresher, sharper. Not quite as heavy. Io trotted over the smoother ground.

"I've never taken Khan here. I wonder if she'd come this far."

"We're making a great loop," said Nigel. "I've ridden Pasha here a few times. If we start veering south, we'll end up by the Petersens'."

"Oh, great. I'm looking forward to seeing them."

Nigel's saddle creaked, but he didn't respond.

"What time is it?"

He peered at his watch. "Almost two."

I stifled a yawn, but even if I were home in bed, I knew I wouldn't sleep.

The horses walked and trotted easily, their legs wet with dew. The wind snapped through the sky, a silent voice. We wound up on an unfamiliar ridge, dark, yet friendly. I put my hands under Io's mane as he jogged, guiding him down off the ridge and through a gully that must have once been a rushing stream when the earth was younger. Io hurried now, his ears up, and he sniffed the air.

Pockets of night clung to the hills, and out of the darkness stepped a figure. Io snorted and propped, his forefeet off the ground in a small, frightened rear.

"Steady," I said, my heart beating faster. "Khan?" My energy surged. What other horse would be in these hills?

"There she is," breathed Nigel. "I can't believe our luck."

Luck? I didn't think so. We came closer, and the horse was backlit by the pale sky, exposing a rider. Someone had found Khan!

"Who's there?" I called. Nigel rode Ariel up beside me.

A loud sniff, then, "It's me. Sarah."

I slumped back, unbelieving. Of all people! I clenched my retainer.

"Sarah, what are you doing?" asked Nigel, not moving. I felt the warmth of his leg against mine.

"Everyone is out looking for you two," she said, as she rode her Thoroughbred closer.

I hadn't even thought about Dad worrying. Nigel's mother worrying. "Has anyone seen Khan?" I asked.

Sarah paused, then said softly, "Yes."

My heart raced. "Where? How bad is she hurt?"

"I don't know. I was afraid to look." Sarah pointed to the underbelly of the ridge, thick with brush. "She's down there. I started down and saw her lying down." Sarah broke off, holding up her hands helplessly, her eyes huge.

I kicked Io and rode him down the trail.

18
Easter Morning

Io couldn't hurry down the narrow, twisted trail. Stones and twigs rolled under his hooves, and he snorted impatiently. How did Sarah find Khan? *Please, don't let it be too late.* If Khan was badly hurt—I couldn't think any further.

The sky had brightened, but the valley was still dark. I leaned close to Io's neck as branches snagged my hair. *God, if You let Khan be all right, I'll be nicer to Sarah.* Bargaining. What did I have to bargain with? Nothing. God did whatever He liked, whether it pleased me or not.

Khan's image rose before me. Silver and proud. And Sarah's image. Golden and proud. I hugged Io's neck, my fingers twined in his long, course mane.

A startling thought charged into my being: Sarah was more important than Khan. *But I love Khan.* So? God loved Sarah more than any horse, more than Khan. I couldn't keep treating Khan better.

Io jogged off the hill and into a grotto, filled with dark green smells. Dampness and moss. Nigel and Sarah rode down behind me. The grotto was rough and uneven from ancient ripples in the earth. Across a patch of grass and low mustard bushes was something pale. Not gray, but white, unlike Khan. It was curled, head down.

Io whickered, and the white creature rasied its head. Next to it lay a gray body—Khan! For a foolish moment I thought she'd had a foal.

The white creature sprang to its legs. An Albino deer!

"Would you look at that," whispered Nigel.

"That's why I was afraid," said Sarah. "I've never seen a white deer."

My mouth dropped. Perhaps it was Farley's unicorn.

With a bound it cleared Khan, who was flat on her side, and bounded through the grass, its tail flicked up in warning.

"Why was it lying with Khan?" asked Sarah.

The deer swept up the opposite hill, paused on the lip of the ridge, and vanished into the darkness.

I slipped off Io and hurried to Khan.

"Khan," I whispered, touching her throat. Her eyes were closed, her nostrils slack. I ran my hand along her mane, sticky with congealed blood. My tears fell on her gray face, mixing with blood and dirt. "Oh, Khan."

Nigel knelt beside me, his hands on her flanks. He took my hand and placed my palm against her flank. It moved slowly, evenly.

"She's not dead," I whispered.

He shook his head. "Unconscious."

We ran our hands over her, lightly touching the scratches and a few deeper cuts. Should I go for a vet? Maybe we should try and rouse her. Her worst cut was on her shoulder.

"Water might revive her," said Nigel.

We hunted for water while Sarah watched our

horses, holding their reins so they didn't go exploring. I found a small pool, dark as a starless night, and scooped some up in the edge of my nylon jacket. I ran back to Khan before it all soaked into the material and dashed it over her face.

At first she didn't move. I turned to get more when she drew in a shuddering sigh. I dropped to my knees. Khan opened her eyes with a surprised snort, as if to say, "What are you doing here?"

"Khan. Good girl," I said and put my cheek against hers. She struggled against me until I moved back. Then she touched me with her soft nose. She lifted her head higher and grunted, rocking her body back and forth.

"Come on, girl," I said and put my hand on her crest. She rolled and thrust her legs out.

"If she can stand, she'll be all right," said Nigel.

Khan heaved herself up, half-grunting, half-squealing, and stood panting, head low. She had a chest wound that I hadn't seen at first, long and ragged, bleeding again from her exertion. Her hocks and knees were banged up, probably from the jump over the wooden fence. I put my arms around her neck, and she pressed her nose against my back.

We led Khan slowly out of the grotto. She limped off her back leg.

"The same leg as before," I said.

"She probably reinjured it," said Nigel. "She made a couple of tremendous leaps."

We rode home through gathering fog. Sarah rode next to Nigel.

"How did you find Khan?" I asked, surprised that my voice sounded so normal.

"I'm not sure," said Sarah. "My dad and your dad sent everyone out looking for you. I rode with your dad for awhile. He's nice." She looked away for a moment, then continued. "We separated, and I was riding along the ridge when something burst out of the bushes. My horse spooked, and he never spooks. Then this thing, whatever it was, took off down into the gully. I thought it was Khan at first, but it was that white deer. Then I saw Khan. I thought she was dead. I rode back to wait at the top for someone to come along."

"An angel unaware," I said.

"Are angels animals?" asked Nigel.

"I don't know. I've never met any kind of angel."

We rested Khan several times. Once I pressed the lining of my jacket against her chest wound to stop the bleeding.

As we rode into the Petersen ranch, a yell cut through the air, and a horseman galloped toward us. Dad. On old Bottom, who raced up the hill toward us, his knee popping..

Dad drew rein. "Thank God, you're safe. And you found her! We were ready to call the search and rescue team. Are you all right?"

Are we all right? I looked at Nigel. We were. I glanced at Sarah, and she met my gaze and looked back unflinchingly. *Are we all right?* We haven't been, but maybe we could be. Sarah gave me a small smile.

"We're all right," I told Dad.

Khan whickered to Bottom. I handed the lead rope to Dad, and he examined her quickly. "She'll be okay, I think," he said. "Let's get her home."

Home. I allowed myself a yawn.

Sarah started her bay down the trail. Nigel and I rode after her, with Dad and Khan behind. The fog was thicker there than in the hills, but I said to Nigel, "It's going to be a bright day."

"Are you crazy? It's foggy."

"But it's Easter. It's always bright on Easter."

159

Nigel shook his head, as though he thought I was crazy, but I saw a small dawning in his eyes.

Easter. Things changed because of Easter. I looked back at Khan, limping behind. Soon the day would be bright. Very bright. Nigel and I grinned at each other. We were all right.